MW00417127

ECHOES

Nancy Morse

A KISMET™ Romance

METEOR PUBLISHING CORPORATION
Bensalem, Pennsylvania

KISMET™ is a trademark of Meteor Publishing Corporation

First Printing March 1992.

ISBN: 1-878702-83-1

Printed in the United States of America

To Talley and to new beginnings!

NANCY MORSE

Born and raised in New York, Nancy now lives in Florida with her husband of 24 years. An early love of reading and happy endings led to the publication of her first romance in 1980. She has an avid interest in American Indian art and culture and takes great pride in her collection of nineteenth century artifacts. Nancy enjoys the simple pleasures of being with friends, seeing good films and relaxing at home, and likes to sweat out daily frustrations through vigorous aerobics workouts.

ONE

The echo of a gunshot ricocheted off the surrounding hills, and a small plug of earth covered in green clover shot into the air. Cal Walker bolted upright from where he was kneeling over the carcass of a sheep; dark hair slashed across his forehead as his head spun around. Whoever shot at him had come dangerously close to hitting him, if that hole in the ground just inches away from his boot was any indication.

His eyes narrowed as they suspiciously hunted the horizon. Beyond the low-lying hills, the Canadian Rockies towered against a sky that was overcast and black. But neither the majestic peaks nor the threatening storm were noticed by Cal, whose gaze was riveted upon a solitary figure standing at the top of a distant rise.

It was too far away to make out the face of the figure on the hillside, but with the combative stance of feet braced apart and the muzzle of a long-range rifle pointed at Cal, the threat was unmistakable.

The thought leapt into Cal's mind to make a run for his pickup truck, which was parked nearby, but common sense rooted him to his spot. Something in his gut told him the bullet had missed him by inches on purpose. Whoever was up there knew how to shoot; to move now would be suicide. There was nothing Cal could do except stand there, his gaze searing back across the darkening distance, and curse to himself as the figure on the hillside slowly lowered the rifle, turned and walked away.

As Cal watched the figure recede over the hill, the aftershocks of fear gave way to rising anger. *Damn those Colemans*, he stormed to himself.

Cal couldn't remember a time when the Walkers and the Colemans hadn't been feuding. Cattlemen and sheep ranchers were natural enemies, after all. But when Angus Coleman had been alive, it had been a clean and honest fight among hardworking men whose misfortune it was to be neighbors. Cal could recall times when the feud had gotten pretty heated, but not a single shot had been fired—until today. He shook his head with disgust. The Coleman place wasn't the same since old Angus had died. If it was bad then, it was worse now.

Cal glanced down at the sheep carcass he'd been examining and grimaced. *Damn those Colemans*, he thought again in rising anger. Their miserable sheep laid to waste good pastureland by grazing the grass down too low. What's more, dead sheep were likely to bring the wolves down out of the high country and force Cal to post double sentries around his own herds of grazing cattle.

Just then, a sliver of pain penetrated Cal's thoughts. Absently, his fingers came up to rub the spot, easing the pain that came at strange and unwelcome times—like now. Beneath his touch, the ridges of a scar were etched into his left cheek beginning at a point below his eye and slashing downward toward his jaw. Sometimes the flesh there felt hot, triggering memories of the accident that had left its mark.

Cal's heart began to thump hard in his chest, as it invariably did whenever he thought about it. It was inevitable. No matter which way his thoughts turned, they always came back to the Colemans. With a bitter taste at the back of his throat he damned them, particularly their dark-eyed women who left scars on the heart as deep as the one on his face.

A rolling clap of thunder resounded in the air, pushing Cal's dismal thoughts aside. He glanced skyward. The clouds were about to burst wide open. If he didn't hurry, he'd be forced to wait out the storm in the cab of the pickup. It wasn't an appealing thought, considering the ferocity of these summer storms. The best Cal could hope for was to find shelter—a stand of pines, an overhang of rock—before it got too bad.

He made a run for it. No sooner did he start up the engine, than the first big drops of rain pelted the windshield. Within minutes Cal was hunched over the steering wheel, trying desperately to see through the curtain of water and cursing the windshield wipers that couldn't keep up with the punishing rain.

Storms like this were common to these turbulent hills and valleys of the Rockies. Cal should have known better than to linger when the sky had been so ominous. He should never have stopped to look at that sheep.

The shock of having been fired at, followed by his

haste to find shelter, had made Cal forget all about the sheep. Only now did he remember what he'd been thinking just as the earth had flown up beside him. There hadn't been a mark on that carcass, nor had the animal shown any signs of starvation.

Cal knew as well as any sheep rancher that, in time, that ewe might have become unable to graze, the erosion of its teeth over the years from constant grazing eventually forcing it into starvation. The chances were good that it would have been slaughtered for mutton, anyway. But Cal's examination had found it to be a healthy female, capable of producing more lambs before her teeth wore out and she became somebody's Sunday dinner. No, something else had killed that ewe.

Cal turned off the road onto a dirt path barely wide enough to accommodate the pickup. With visibility limited to only a few feet at best, he steered for a place he remembered. What prompted him to think of it at this precise moment was unclear to him.

The roughly-hewn line shack had been built by some nameless rancher for warmth and dryness while tending the herds in winter long before Cal was born. Cal used to go there as a boy, having discovered the place one day while out riding. With the possible exception of one other person whom he preferred *not* to think of, no one else knew its location.

He hadn't seen the place in years. Someone had most likely chopped it up for firewood a long time ago, or else the timbers had rotted away with age. It was possible that old line shack no longer existed.

For that reason Cal was not only surprised but suspicious when the yellow beams of his headlights sliced across a vehicle parked out front. He brought the pickup to a halt alongside it. He recognized with disapproval the Coleman station wagon. Cal made a dash for the door, cursing his luck at finding the shack—*his* shack—occupied by someone from the Coleman place.

It was the sound of silence in the wake of all that thunder and lightning that made Catherine stir in her slumber. She awakened gradually so her thoughts were in motion and her senses were alert before her eyes were even open.

There came to her the smell of damp earth and the sound of water dripping through a hole in the roof. Familiar odors and friendly sounds lulled her into a state of semi-contentment. And for the time being, the events that brought her back to this place were forgotten.

Uncurling her fingers, she splayed them against the ground on which she lay. The earth was cool and dry to the touch. From it she determined that the sun was on its way down. Ten years was a long time to be away, but Angus had taught her well. She didn't have to open her eyes to know that the sky outside was fired up with the brilliant pinks and oranges of twilight in the aftermath of the storm, nor see the creeks to know that they were overflowing from the heavy rains. The memory of it was as familiar to her as the fierce black sky and ominous thunder that had sent her scurrying for shelter.

Shelter. Wasn't that what she had come back to Alberta for? Shelter from the storm of emotions following a bitter divorce?

The summers she had spent on her grandfather's sheep ranch in western Canada had led Catherine to regard this place as home. This was where she'd been happiest as a child. This was where that happiness had come crashing to an end ten years ago. Ironically, this was where she ran to now, when there was no place else to go.

The past decade had led Catherine on a circuitous route as the wife of a powerful American businessman. Then, from a courtroom of the United States Southern District Court in one of the most publicized divorce cases America had seen in years, full circle back to the Canadian province of Alberta. To the crumbling sheep ranch of her youth and a shack in the middle of nowhere that only she, and possibly one other person, knew existed.

Catherine recalled the vow never to return she'd made ten years earlier. Except for that brief time she'd come back for Angus's funeral, she'd almost kept that vow. But circumstances made that solemn vow seem now like mere words. Here she was, practically broke, having used up the inheritance her father left her to buy her freedom from an unhappy marriage, with a neglected, almost-bankrupt sheep ranch on her hands.

The joke was on her it seemed, but that was all right as far as Catherine was concerned. Up here, she could be just plain Catherine Coleman—Angus wouldn't mind if she borrowed his last name—instead of Catherine Randolph, daughter of Boston tycoon Ellis Randolph, or Catherine Chandler, wife of a man whose philandering was as famous as the hotels and office towers he built. Up here, in the vast Canadian wilderness, it was easy to get lost in obscurity. The newsmen and photographers who'd hounded her during the divorce proceedings would not find her here. But perhaps, she reasoned, she could find herself, for she seemed to have lost track of herself somewhere along the way.

She wished her grandfather were still alive. He would have chided her for coming back, but he would have understood. She was just grateful that there was a place to come back to.

With that small but comforting thought in mind, Catherine sighed and stirred, drifting in and out of memories, unaware of the eyes that were watching her from the shadows.

Cal could tell by the sound of her breathing that she was awake even though her lids were still lowered. He watched her in silence, tracing with his eyes the line of her profile against the growing darkness. The soft, curving line of her silhouette, the shadowed profile. Even in the dark it was plain to see that she was as beautiful as he remembered. To his own self-disgust he found himself hating her for it.

He knew now who had shot at him earlier. If old Angus Coleman had taught his granddaughter anything, it was how to shoot. Cal could recall trying to best her at fifty paces, but she'd beaten him every time. Little had he known back then, when they'd been two kids shooting at tin cans, that she would one day shoot at him in earnest.

"Do you always shoot at people like that?"

Catherine's eyes snapped open at the masculine voice that spoke from somewhere close by. In those few words she heard the anger and hostility of the speaker. In that initial instant before her body reacted, it registered upon her brain that the voice sounded familiar. Every muscle in Catherine's body tensed.

It was dark in the small line shack. Dusk threw long shadows across the walls of rotting timber. Catherine's eyes adjusted rapidly to the absence of light. She gasped to see the figure of a man sitting on the ground.

He sat with his back pressed against a splintered wall. One leg was stretched out across the earth floor. The other knee was drawn up, with one arm slung across it. His face was in profile, the half that was visible cloaked in shadow. But even if Catherine had possessed no sight at all, she would have known him.

Her heart slammed against the wall of her chest with instant recognition. She'd had no idea who that was she'd spotted kneeling over one of her sheep. She'd thought to fire a close shot to warn the intruder that his presence in her pasture wasn't welcome, little knowing that the echo of her gunshot would reverberate clear to the past and back to this moment. The familiar ring of that voice forced Catherine's throat to constrict so tightly that not a single sound emerged.

"Hello, Cathy."

There it was again, this time reluctantly softer, its deepness stirring memories. Catherine's own voice scratched painfully at the back of her throat. Somehow she managed a reply.

"Hello, Cal."

For several minutes after that neither of them spoke. At length the silence became overbearing. Catherine rose shakily to her feet, brushed herself off, and stood there self-consciously, not knowing what to say. What *could* she say to a man she hadn't seen or heard from in ten years?

"Do you always tresspass on other people's land?"

"When there's a storm about to break and I need to take a shortcut, I do."

"How long—?" Her voice cracked. She cleared her throat and began again. "How long have you been sitting there?"

Long enough for the sight of her to tighten a knot in his belly, Cal thought with dismay. He gestured toward the window with a flick of the head and said, "Storm's over."

Catherine glanced anxiously at the window. "The storm. Yes. It came from out of nowhere."

Cal snorted derisively and said, "They usually do at this time of year," adding flatly, "I'm surprised you don't remember that." Apparently, there were a lot of things she didn't remember, or else chose to forget. Either way, he told himself it made no difference to him. Affecting a disinterested tone, he asked, "So, what brings you back to these parts, Cathy?"

To Catherine his question carried the annoying ring of I-told-you-so. Wearily she replied, "It's a long story." And one she had no intention of going into with him, of all people.

He went on in a deceptively casual tone that should have warned her they were headed for dangerous waters. "I seem to recall that when you left here—what was it, oh, ten years ago?—you said you were never coming back."

She stiffened at the reminder. "How would you know what I said when you weren't around to hear it?"

He should have known that she would respond without backing down. Wasn't it just like her, even now after all these years, to challenge him as if it had been yesterday? Cal shifted uncomfortably in his seated position on the ground. Back then, word had reached him that she'd left for good.

He only wondered why word had not reached him now that she'd come back. Why did he have to find out like this, as if he'd stuck his finger into a socket and ten thousand volts of electricity had shot through him?

He knew why she'd come back. He'd read about her divorce in the Edmonton papers and had felt a small twist of triumph to learn of the demise of her marriage. The accompanying photograph had also not been without its impact. It had been a shot of Cathy coming out of the courthouse after the divorce had been granted. Those dark, serious eyes, the full lips compressed into a tense smile for the clicking shutters of the photographers' cameras. Her somber beauty had appealed to him against his will as much then as it always had . . . as much as it did right now.

Cal galvanized himself against it. "What happened?" he asked. "Got tired of all that fancy living and decided to come back to the family sheep ranch?"

Catherine responded to his pointed sarcasm by observing, "You sound as if you resent my having a place to come back to, Cal."

It wasn't the coming back he resented; it was the leaving in the first place. "Why the sudden interest in sheep?" he pressed.

"Because now they're *my* sheep."

It was true, they were her sheep, but when Angus died and left the ranch to her, she had never planned on coming back to run it. What she didn't say was that not a day had gone by these past ten years that she had not thought of this place, or of him, in one way or another.

"This place is in my blood," she said. "I guess I'm Angus Coleman's granddaughter, after all."

"Yeah," muttered Cal. "And Ellis Randolph's daughter, too." The bitterness behind those softly spoken words made Catherine shudder.

Her father, having hated sheep ranching with a vengence, had kept to his own domain of trading in international markets. From the pinnacle of his Boston office tower, he'd been unaware of his daughter's summer romance with the son of the neighboring cattle rancher until Catherine had announced her intention to marry Calvin Walker. Ellis had flown into a rage. Catherine had been summoned home from Alberta for a severe upbraiding, only to race back to Cal in defiance of her father's wishes. When she got there, however, Cal was gone. Neither Angus nor anyone else could tell her where he'd gone, or more important, why.

One year later Catherine married someone else, never suspecting that her father may have played a role in orchestrating the outcome. All she knew then, or now, was that she had been betrayed by Cal.

Himself unaware of the external forces that may have had a hand in shaping his life, Cal knew only that having been in love with Ellis Randolph's daughter once had nearly destroyed him. He wasn't about to make that mistake again.

"It's going to take a lot of hard work to save that place," he said. "I hear it's gotten pretty rundown since Angus died."

Catherine shrugged against the growing darkness. "I learned a few things about sheep ranching from my grandfather. And what I don't know, I'm sure my foreman does."

From out of the shadows came a deep laugh. "It's too bad your foreman doesn't know anything about boundary lines."

"What's that supposed to mean?"

He took his time answering, rising to his feet first and stretching the lean muscles in his back and legs while keeping to the velvet darkness. "Ask your foreman about it."

It wasn't that Catherine had forgotten how tall and broad-shouldered Cal was. It was just that she had underestimated the impact it would have on her. When he'd been seated on the ground, she had somehow felt more in control than she now suddenly did. She watched him warily and, in spite of herself, admiringly.

The years had added flatteringly to Cal's appeal. As a boy, he'd been lean and wiry, like a spring in motion. As a young man, he'd exuded athletic prowess. But this was no boy standing before her, no young man on the threshold of uncovering his ultimate strength. This was a man full grown, handsome, and hostile, a dangerous combination under any circumstances.

"That was one of your sheep I found out there today, dead."

Catherine pushed aside her disturbing thoughts of him and responded with an even tone. "I'm sure there's a logical explanation for it. Sheep don't die for no reason. Maybe its teeth—"

"Its teeth were fine," Cal cut in.

"Wolves, then."

"Wolves didn't kill it. A wolf would have dragged it off."

"You seem pretty certain as to what *didn't* kill it," she said. "Care to venture a guess as to what did?"

Cal shrugged with indifference. "Who knows?"

"Something could be contaminating the water further upstream," she ventured, adding purposefully, "Or some*one*."

He looked at her skeptically. "Who would want to kill your sheep?"

Parodying his indifference, she quipped. "Who knows? Maybe some cattle rancher with a gripe."

His features remained unreadable, indeed scarcely visible from where he stood. If he was surprised by the remark, she saw no outward sign of it.

Inside of Cal, however, much was going on. He was shocked that she thought him capable of killing her sheep. He figured it only went to show how little he knew her. It was ironic, for there was a time when he thought he knew her so well. That, of course, had been before their bubble had burst and they'd been hurled into separate orbits, only to come crashing to earth ten years later, each landing in a small wooden shack deep in the Alberta foothills. No, he wasn't surprised by the remark, only deeply disappointed by it.

"I have no reason to kill your sheep, Cathy."

She regretted saying it the instant the words had formed on her lips, but the sound of Cal's voice now, filled with anger and pain, only made Catherine feel worse.

She went to the window and looked out. It was nightfall. Overhead a crescent moon appeared through the feathery branches of the pines. The stars were out, and all that remained of the previous storm was the smell of damp grass. She breathed in the sweet night aroma.

She knew she ought to be getting back. Even though she had assured Gertie, the housekeeper, that she knew her way around the hills and valleys, she was bound to be looked upon as a newcomer to these parts and easily capable of getting lost in a storm. The last thing she wanted to do was worry Gertie needlessly, or to give Ben, her foreman, reason to think that she wasn't cut out to run the ranch. He wasn't, after all, the friendliest person in the first place.

Yet, while Catherine's better judgment told her she should be going, she dared not budge, not with Cal watching her from the shadows with predatory eyes. He was keeping his distance, but that was fine as far as she was concerned. The air around him sizzled with hostility, and she had no wish to get any closer. What was he so angry at? she wondered. If anyone had a right to be angry, it was she. She was the one who'd been jilted. Perhaps the guilt had become too much for him. Well, what did he expect? No one got off scot-free. In one way or another, it always came back to haunt you.

Something had, indeed, come back to haunt Cal Walker. He had closed his mind to her, shut her out of his heart. But to his shock and utter dismay, the years had not taught his body how to stop wanting her. Now, as then, it reacted with a predictable longing. Feeling betrayed by his own body, he told himself it was just the way any red-blooded man would react to a beautiful woman. And she was certainly that.

A ribbon of pale moonlight fell softly upon her face as she stood at the window. A sheen of perspiration had evaporated from her skin, giving her complexion a matte look. Smooth, flawless, and as Cal remembered only too well, remarkably soft to the touch.

Her dark hair hung free. She had never cared for styling it, and while it was shorter than it used to be, reaching now to her shoulders instead of her waist, Cal was pleased to see that she still preferred to wear it loose and casual. His fingers flexed involuntarily at his sides. They knew the feeling of being buried in the deep, dark fullness of her hair.

Those eyes that had always reminded him of semisweet chocolate were focused out the window. She looked to be a thousand miles away, yet Cal knew that she was very much aware of him. The carefree, unrestrained girl who could ride with the best of them and shoot better than any of them was now a carefully-guarded woman whose mistrust was evident in her dark eyes.

He couldn't blame her, he supposed. It couldn't have been easy for someone as strong-willed as Cathy to be the daughter of a tyrant like Ellis Randolph; or for a woman of such spirit and emotion as the one he remembered to adjust easily to life as the wife of a man like the one she had married. Be that as it may, he had the distinct feeling that it was neither her father nor her ex-husband with whom she was angry, but him. Cal's defenses went up. He was the one who should be angry, damnit, and he was!

Why shouldn't he be? He's the one who'd been left with a broken heart.

The air inside the tiny shack grew thick with tension in the ensuing silence. The distance between them was riddled with mistrust and suspicion. And yet, in spite of themselves, something endured, transcending the miles and the years, causing a tiny spark to ignite.

Catherine heaved a sigh of resignation, thinking dismally how some things never change. She'd always been shamefully attracted to Cal. Sadly, in spite of everything, she still was. She turned from the window and walked to the door.

As he watched her go, Cal snorted with self-disgust and told himself it was hormonal. Stay, he ordered himself. Don't follow her. But even as he thought it, his body was in motion.

Outside, the ground was soft from the rain. The soil smelled rich and sweet. The night was warm and clear.

Catherine walked to her car and fished into the pocket of her jeans for the keys. She heard Cal's footsteps come up behind her, and tensed. A part of her wished she had never come back. The best thing would be to get into the car and drive away without saying another word. What was there to say, anyway, except to ask why?

Too often over the years she had thought of him and asked herself why. Why he'd been gone when she got back. Even now, as she fumbled with the door, that one word echoed through her mind.

Cal expected Catherine to get into the car and drive away. He half wished she would. He moved past her toward the pickup, never anticipating that she would turn to him suddenly the way she did, as if to say something, only to freeze with her mouth open.

It was the way the moonlight struck his face that rendered Catherine speechless and caused the muscles in her body to go rigid. For the first time she saw him clearly, distinctly.

Those hazel eyes of his that hedged somewhere between light brown and green were fixed anxiously on her. His dark hair fell over his forehead in a crop of unruly curls and looked to be in need of a trim at the collar. Dark stubble spiked his chin. More than one day's growth, she surmised from the look of it.

The years had sharpened the angles of his face and etched tiny lines around the corners of his changeable eyes. His was a careless, haphazard handsomeness that, for some reason, had always appealed to her. Her eyes swept over his face. In the very next instant, he turned his head and she saw it.

Catherine's gasp at the sight of the scar, although only a whisper, ripped through Cal like the jagged edge of a blade. Her hand flew out to him and in a shortened breath she whispered his name.

Cal braced himself for an onrush of pity and jerked away, freezing Catherine in mid-motion just shy of physical contact. He dismissed her shock gruffly by saying, "It's nothing."

"But, Cal, how—?"

"Forget it," he said. "It was an accident. It happened a long time ago."

The accompanying flash from his eyes warned Catherine not to press the issue. Whoever or whatever had put that scar on Cal's cheek was clearly not a subject he wanted to speak about.

Catherine's moment of genuine concern left her feeling angry and confused, but most of all foolish. She climbed into the car and for several moments sat there, regrouping. The unexpected reunion with Cal had left her shaken. She'd come to Alberta to get away from her problems, not add to them.

Cal's sharp rap on the window made Catherine jump. She rolled the glass down and looked up into his unsmiling face. From this angle the scar on his cheek looked like a cavern. It was frightening and, in a strange unsettling way, compelling.

"You'd do best to pick that carcass up first thing in the morning and get it over to a vet's for an autopsy. The quicker you know what killed her, the better."

She cringed at the know-it-all tone of voice. "I'll take care of it." She leaned forward to start up the engine, but Cal's hand clamped down on her shoulder. With fingers flexing strongly against her flesh, he pulled her back against the seat. Her gaze flew up to his.

"I mean it, Cathy," he warned. "Anything could have killed that ewe. Maybe the water's contaminated. If it is, I've got to know. That water passes through your land on its way to mine. If you don't do something about it, I will."

Catherine's own glare stuck bravely to his as she issued a warning of her own. "Calvin Walker, don't you dare."

It wasn't the command that made Cal turn to ice inside. It was the vivid memory it conjured up in his mind of a pretty, dark-eyed girl shaking a finger at him and warning him in that same tone of voice, Calvin Walker, don't you dare.

The years seemed to shrink before Cal's eyes. For one monstrously brief moment, it was as if nothing had changed. It hit him harder than he expected, and long after the red glow of her tail lights had disappeared into the darkness, all he could do was stand there and remember.

TWO

At a place where the western prairie met the foothills of the Rockies, nestled in a bend of the Little Smoky River, a rakish assembly of buildings and corrals lay smothered in the August heat. It was a drab and dusty place, where bleating sheep chorused with barking dogs and the musty odor of fleece hung heavy over everything, mingling with the dust in the wind. Overhead, a blistering sun turned the grass dry and shortened tempers.

In the west corral two figures worked among the flock, singling out animals to be vaccinated. The last sheep to receive the antibiotic bleated with indignation and ran off into the fold.

Since Catherine's return, several sheep had turned up missing from the flocks and were presumed dead. Having grown up around sheep, she knew it could be any number of things—natural causes, contaminated water, a viral infection. The absence of carcasses posed no immediate cause for concern, for scavenging wolves and coyotes were known to carry off full-grown sheep. Vaccinating the flocks was a precaution she could not afford not to take.

Ben McFarland wiped his hands on his pants and said confidently, "That oughta do it."

Catherine ran a bare arm across her brow to catch the glistening droplets of perspiration that fell into her lashes and said gravely, "Let's hope so."

With a shrug that suggested to Catherine that he shared neither her concern nor her opinion, Ben replied, "I guess it can't hurt."

Ben McFarland was a man in his mid-forties who had taken on the job of running the ranch when Angus died, having answered the advertisement Catherine had placed in *The Edmonton News* for a foreman. Over the years he sent her regular reports. From them she knew that the ranch was not prospering, but until she arrived and saw it for herself, she'd had no idea how bad things really were. Cal was right. It was going to take a lot of hard work to save this place.

Working with a disgruntled foreman didn't make things any easier. Catherine squinted her eyes against the glare of the sun to see him better. This wasn't the first time she had detected an undisguised indifference in Ben's manner. She attributed it to his apprehension over her having come back to run things. It couldn't be easy for him, she surmised, sharing the running of the ranch with her after six years of doing it on his own.

Her gaze moved past Ben to sweep the sun-hazed surroundings. Fences needed mending. The roof of the shearing shed was crying out for repair. From the look of things, Ben needed all the help he could get.

She turned back to him and said solemnly, "We can't afford to lose any more sheep."

"Sheep die," he said. "You gotta expect to lose a few head each season. We lost half a dozen in a blizzard last winter."

It was hot and Catherine was rapidly losing patience, not only with the day, but with Ben. "Yes, they die. From bad winters, from illness, from difficult births, from wolves and coyotes, from any number of things. But when they die for no apparent reason, I find that rather curious." Her dark eyes regarded him closely. "Don't you?"

He responded defensively, "We're doing the best we can with what we've got."

Catherine expelled a breath of frustration. "You're right, Ben. I'm sorry."

He accepted the apology as if it was his due. "If you don't mind my saying, what we need is money."

Catherine laughed in spite of herself. "You make it sound so simple."

"Well, isn't it, for someone like you?"

"Why should it be?"

"Well, uh . . ." He grew uncomfortable beneath her steady stare. "You come from a rich family, and—"

She interrupted him with another laugh, only this time the sound was without humor. "Sorry, Ben, I'm broke." She didn't want to tell him that she had used the inheritance her father left her to buy her freedom from an unhappy marriage. "We'll just have to find another way to get the money we need to stay in business."

In the few weeks he'd known her, Ben found Catherine to be a strong-minded and stubborn woman. He knew by now when to drop an issue. Yet she also possessed a paradoxical nature that invariably took him by surprise, as it did in the very next instant when the flash of annoyance he'd just seen in her dark eyes was quickly diminished by a soft chuckle.

"It's too bad it's sheep and not oil, huh, Ben?"

He was taken off guard by the unexpected and somewhat poignant humor. "There's always that old rig up in the northeast quarter," he said in jest.

With a mixture of fondness and regret, Catherine remembered her grandfather's one-and-only attempt at drilling for oil.

Angus had sworn by the drilling reports and vowed to drill clear to China. Ellis, however, had laughed at his father-in-law's venture, claiming there wasn't any oil beneath Angus's land. And who would know better than Ellis Randolph, a man who made his fortune exploiting the oil resources of a country that wasn't even his own?

The story was local history. It began in 1942 when the threat of a Japanese invasion proved to the United States that an overland route to Alaska was necessary. Within months, the Alaska Highway spanned five mountain ranges and the wilderness. American servicemen, Ellis Randolph among them, flooded into Edmonton, which had become the center for northern United States military operations.

After the war, Ellis stayed on. He married pretty Mary Coleman, Angus's daughter, and bought some land. In 1945, just south of town, Leduc Number 1 became the first major oil discovery north of Turner Valley. It was followed by Pembina, Woodbend, and

Redwater. But it was the discovery of huge crude reserves in a forty-acre tar sand owned by Ellis Randolph that made the record books.

From there, Ellis parlayed his fortune into more land and more oil wells. Pumping "grasshoppers" dotted his fields, and he became one of the wealthiest men in Alberta. He had liked to boast that he'd been in the right place at the right time when, in fact, he had orchestrated every move that led to his fame and fortune. Eventually, he turned away from the land that made him rich. American by birth, it was there that he built his vast conglomerate, collecting politicians and judges the way other men collect stamps.

It was no wonder that Ellis had scoffed at Angus's pitiful venture, or that he had refused the Scotsman's request for a loan to drill the well. In the end, Angus's hopes, like his well, dried up.

Catherine sighed with the memory of the rig up in the northeast quarter and said regretfully, "That old well's as dry as a bone."

Ben muttered something about it being too bad as the two of them walked from the corral and followed the dirt path that led back to the house.

"I want you to keep your eyes open," said Catherine. "If you find any dead sheep, I want them brought in immediately." She still couldn't figure out what happened to that carcass she'd spotted the day of the storm. When she'd gone back for it the next day, it had been gone.

"I told you," said Ben. "Coyotes got it."

"There were no tracks," Catherine argued.

"The rain must have washed them away."

She drew in an uncertain breath. "Maybe you're

right." She fell into silent thought for a moment, then said, "Tell me, Ben, is Doctor Devlin practicing?"

"Sure. He's in Edmonton."

Doc Devlin was probably in his eighties by now, but he was someone Catherine remembered from the old days, someone she could trust among all these strangers. "Good. The next dead sheep we find goes straight to Doc Devlin. We'll let a veterinarian determine what killed it."

From there the conversation turned to overdue bills and matters pertaining to the everyday running of the ranch as they walked the rest of the way to the house.

The house Angus Coleman built of stone and weathered timber was situated at the top of a rise that overlooked a valley of spruce and fir. As they rounded the corner, the land sloped away, exposing the panoramic valley below. Catherine smiled in spite of her mood. The scene was perfect. The only thing missing was Angus himself.

Into her mind sprang the image of her grandfather standing on the porch, a pipe between his lips, listening gravely the day she told him she was leaving and never coming back. Devastated by Cal's betrayal, she had spilled her tears onto her grandfather's shirt while he, in his soft lilting brogue, told her that she was wrong about Cal. He'd spoken to Cal himself, he'd said. Cal would come back. But Cal *didn't* come back, not for many long years, and in the end even Angus was forced to admit he'd been wrong.

Catherine pulled in a ragged breath. It was impossible to think of Cal without experiencing a pang of the old bitterness. Her father used to say that every man has his price. Where Cal Walker was concerned, apparently he was right.

The steps creaked as Catherine and Ben climbed them to the front door. Masking her interest behind a level tone, she asked, "Ben, what do you know about Cal Walker?"

"You mean over at Pitchfork? Not very much," he answered as he followed her through the screen door.

"When did he come back to Pitchfork?"

"Can't say exactly. He was there when I came to work for you, and that was what, six, six-and-a-half years ago?"

That would be around the time Angus died, thought Catherine. She wondered whether Angus had known of Cal's return.

"Do you know the guy?" Ben asked.

She did once, a long time ago, she thought, but now? "No," she answered, "I don't know him. Do you?"

"I met him a couple of times. They've got this annual barbecue over at Pitchfork. The first year we were here, me and Gertie went over."

The memory of the Pitchfork barbecues was firmly etched in Catherine's mind. She remembered vividly how she and Cal used to slip away from the grown-ups and run off, sometimes for a gallop through the valley, or for a shooting contest up in the hills where the echo of their gunshots reached clear to the mountains and back.

"That Walker," said Ben, shaking his head, "there's something strange about him."

Catherine looked up from her private recollections. "Oh? Like what?"

"I don't know. It's the eyes, I think. The way they look at you as if they can see right through you. And he's got this real nasty scar on his face. Me and Gertie left early that day. We never bothered to go to any of the other barbecues after that."

"You said you met him a couple of times."

"Yeah. There was one other time. I was out mending a fence along the boundary where this place meets his. He comes riding up real hard, telling me that the fence is on his property and he wants it off. He gets down and starts pacing off. Tells me if I don't believe him to go to city hall and check it out. The next day I drove into Edmonton to the county courthouse."

So, that was the boundary dispute to which Cal had referred.

"And?"

"He was right."

"What'd you do?"

"What else? I moved the fence."

In the kitchen they found Ben's wife, Gertie, at the counter preparing for dinner. At the sight of their sunburned faces and tired looks, she poured two glasses of lemonade. Ben took a big swallow of his and wiped his mouth with the back of his hand, saying to Catherine as he did, "There's no way I want to mess with that guy. There's something dangerous about him."

At the counter where she was chopping and dicing, Gertie turned a round face at them from over her shoulder and inquired, "Something dangerous about who?"

"We were just talking about that Walker fellow," her husband explained.

"He's not dangerous," said Gertie. "He's just lonely, that's all. It's there in the eyes. I saw it just once and I'll never forget it. He's got this nasty scar on his face, too, which probably scares the women away. That must account for the reason he's still a bachelor." She shook her head sadly and went back to her work. "It's a shame. Without that scar, he'd be such a handsome man."

Ben turned back to Catherine and issued a curt warning. "I'd just stay away from him if I were you."

She bristled at the unfriendly tone. Nevertheless, staying away was exactly what she planned to do, and so far she was succeeding. She hadn't seen Cal since the day of the storm and that was over two weeks ago. To avoid thoughts of him she threw herself into the ranch, working long hours balancing the books, administering to the flocks, tracking inventories, trying to squeeze every penny out of the flagging business. She'd lost five pounds since she arrived with little to show for it.

But if the days were hard, the nights were harder, particularly the hours of sleeplessness during which she tossed and turned, unable to escape the thought of him. It was especially bad at night when the place where his hand had touched her shoulder still throbbed. She should have hated him for the effect he had on her, but she had only herself to blame. Even now, she could not contain her curiosity about him.

In six and a half years Ben McFarland had seen their neighbor only twice. Gertie had seen him only once. Cal was obviously keeping to himself. The discreet questions Catherine asked about him shed little light on what he'd been doing these past ten years or why he chose to live alone. Her imagination piqued by the solitary man, she toyed with the ice cubes in her glass with the tip of a finger and wondered aloud, "Where do you suppose he got that scar on his face?"

"I don't know," said Ben. "Talk is he got it when he was wildcatting up north some years ago, but no one really knows." He turned to his wife and asked, "What's for dinner?"

Gertie's reply was overidden by the sound of a car horn blasting outside and the screech of rapidly approaching tires. Their heads spun in unison in the direction of the open window. Catherine went and looked out. She heard Ben mutter behind her, "Speak of the devil."

Sure enough, something lurched inside Catherine when she recognized Cal's pickup truck barreling up the road toward the house.

They were waiting on the front porch when the pickup came to a sharp halt. The door flew open and Cal stormed out. The warm sunshine glinted off his dark hair as he strode forward with long and purposeful strides. His face was fixed in a scowl. He was wearing jeans and a faded denim shirt whose sleeves were pushed up past the elbows as if he meant business.

In broad daylight the scar on Cal's face gave him a savage look. And whatever foolish romantic notions Catherine had entertained about it when it was cloaked in shadow and moonlight were summarily dispelled in the harsh light of day. Some unknown thing had left a wicked reminder on Cal, casting an imperfect edge to his good looks. Catherine's resolve not to let it affect her shattered like glass in that first instant. To her utter amazement and shame, she could not help but look away.

Cal reached the porch and stopped dead in his tracks to glare up at the two figures who stood at the wooden railing. There was a look of questioning belligerence on Ben McFarland's face. Catherine's gaze was pointedly averted. Cal knew why. The flesh on his cheek felt suddenly hot and he knew it had nothing to do with the sun.

The air sizzled with expectancy as Catherine fixed her eyes upon the weathered timbers at her feet and bore up bravely under Cal's stare. But as the seconds ticked by, each one feeling like eternity, she was faced with the dismal realization that it was useless to avoid him. If it was not his eyes that haunted her as they were doing right now, then it was his memory. Reluctantly, but inevitably, her gaze came up to meet his. For several furious seconds their eyes locked upon each other.

Ben took a step past Catherine and said, "Is there something we can do for you, Walker?"

The tension snapped like a dry twig underfoot. Catherine spoke up. "It's all right, Ben. You go on back to the corral. I'll see to Mr. Walker."

Ben hesitated. His gaze shifted from Catherine to Cal and back again before he complied.

When he was gone, Catherine moved to the edge of the porch, careful to keep her distance from the man who stood in an arrogant stance before her. "What brings you here, Cal?"

He wasn't really sure why he'd come. He told himself it had nothing to do with wanting to see her again. He was angry over her sudden and unwelcome reappearance in his life. He'd gotten little sleep these past two weeks since seeing her again. He supposed that the reason he'd come here this afternoon was to force a confrontation, to put this matter between them to rest once and for all if they were going to be neighbors.

The screen door squeaked on its hinges, sparing Cal the necessity of a reply. Gertie appeared carrying a tray with a pitcher of lemonade and two glasses, which she set down on a small table by the door.

Catherine gave her housekeeper a thankless look. Obliged now to offer Cal a drink, she poured the frosty liquid into a glass and held it out to him. To her chagrin, he climbed the stairs and accepted it.

The glass was cold and wet. He placed it against his forehead as he watched her pour a glass of lemonade for herself. Her movements were graceful as always, confident in a way that had always thrilled him. His own confidence was shaken, however, when she turned to face him and her eyes went at once to his scar. A part of him wanted to turn his face away so that she could not see it. A deeper, darker part of him wanted her to see it so that she would know what she had done.

He took a sip of the cool, sweet drink and went to stand at the porch railing, where he looked out onto the valley spread below them. How many days had he stood here like this with her, drinking fresh lemonade, talking, laughing, just being happy together? How many nights had he come calling and they had watched the sun fire up the western sky behind the peaks?

Caught up in remembering, Cal was finding it difficult to sustain his anger. His coming here today had been an act of pure impulse, but it was impossible to be this close to her and remain detached. The cold, wet drink soothed his thirst, but a familiar hunger continued to gnaw at him.

Cal turned away from the valley and his own empty longings and said, "I presume you did something about that dead sheep."

The glass froze in Catherine's hand midway to her lips. A check of the water had proven it to be free of contamination. She didn't want to admit it to Cal, but her concern was growing. Ruling out water contamination narrowed the possibilities, but what was left was not pleasant. Indirectly, she replied, "I'm taking the proper precautions. Ben and I worked all morning vaccinating the flocks. It's probably a viral infection. The antibiotics should do it."

"Why guess? You could find out once and for all by having that carcass autopsied. You did go back for it, didn't you?"

"Of course, I did." What she didn't say, of course, was that the carcass was gone, and without a carcass there could be no autopsy. She sipped her lemonade, affecting a confidence she didn't really feel. "Everything's under control."

He studied her in the bright sunshine. The ends of her dark hair blew up in the summer breeze. One burnished strand tangled in her lashes. Absently, she reached a bare arm up to brush it away. The unhurried, unrehearsed motion produced a provocative effect. The cotton tank top she was wearing was matted to her flesh in places with perspiration, drawing Cal's eyes like magnets. Feeling suddenly awkward, he swallowed down the rest of his lemonade, walked to the table, and set the empty glass down on the tray.

When he returned to the railing, she was leaning forward on her elbows, staring at the panorama. He leaned forward beside her, their shoulders barely touching.

To the east the rolling parkland stretched clear to the boundary of the Northwest Territories. To the west the colossal shifts and thrusts of the Rockies were set against the blue Alberta sky.

Catherine took a deep breath. The air that flowed into her lungs was hot and dry. With it came the scent of the man beside her, the heady mingling of male musk and sweat. The aroma brought back a million unwanted memories.

"It doesn't change, does it?" she ventured.

"What doesn't?"

You. Me. No matter how hard we try, she was tempted to say. Instead, she gestured to everything around them and said, "All that out there."

"The mountains haven't changed," said Cal. "But everything else around them sure has. Have you seen Edmonton since you've been back?"

"No. I've been busy here. And . . ." She hedged. "To tell you the truth, I've been avoiding the publicity."

He looked at her profile etched against the vibrant blue sky. Something in the candor of her remark touched him. His guard began to slip. "You wouldn't recognize it. That little Italian restaurant we used to go to on Jasper is gone. There's an office building there now." He shrugged fatalistically. "That's progress, I guess."

"That's oil," she corrected.

They both remembered what it was like in the sixties and seventies when the development of huge crude oil reserves was made feasible by rising oil prices. Mega projects were put into operation to reap the oily black harvest, causing the meteoric rise of Edmonton as a world energy and financial center. But the effects of economic recession and declining world oil prices had left their marks on Edmonton, just as past mistakes and misunderstandings had left their marks on the two people who stood in silence at the porch railing.

Catherine straightened up and said, "I have to get back to the flocks."

"Oh yeah, sure. I've got to be getting back, too."

She walked him to his pickup. "Well, Cal, I'll see you around sometime." She turned to go, wanting to say more but not knowing where to begin.

Cal yanked open the door and was about to get in, but stopped. "Cathy," he called to her.

She turned back. Her heart beat a little faster. "Yes?"

"The, uh, the barbecue. You remember, the one we used to have each year at Pitchfork? It's a week from Sunday. I thought maybe you'd like to . . . I mean, maybe you, that is, if you're not doing anything . . ."

It wasn't like Cal, usually so arrogant and outspoken, to be at such a loss for words. Something softened inside of Catherine to see it. Nevertheless, she hesitated with uncertainty. Attending the Pitchfork barbecue was sure to arouse many unwanted memories.

Growing impatient at her silence, Cal scoffed, "In case you're worried about it, nobody need know there was ever anything between us."

She winced at the hard edge of his tone. "That's

right,'' she said flippantly. ''Besides, there certainly isn't anything between us anymore.''

''Right. So?''

''Sure, why not? I'll be there a week from Sunday.''

''You do remember how to get there, don't you?''

Bristling at the unnecessary sarcasm, she replied, ''I remember a lot of things.''

''No kidding. Hell, Cathy, the way you lit out of here ten years ago I figured you must have struck your head on something and clean forgotten everything.''

He was smiling, but Catherine knew better than to take it as a harmless joke. She tilted her face up at him, defying the flutter in her stomach that came each time she looked into those hazel eyes. Refusing, too, to be cowed by the scar on his face. Tersely, she replied, ''Not quite everything, Cal. It's hard to forget, for instance, just what twenty-five thousand dollars will buy.'' There, she thought, it was out. Let him dare to deny it!

Cal glared at her as if she'd gone insane. For one terrible instant, Catherine thought she had gone too far. Finally, he tore his gaze away, got into the truck and started up the engine. ''A week from Sunday,'' he said. Thrusting the gearshift into first, he peeled away in mounting anger.

Cal had not driven more than a quarter of a mile and already he was regretting his actions. What on earth had possessed him to drive over there today, much less invite her to Pitchfork? Was he out of his mind? Worse, her reference to the twenty-five thousand dollars made him seethe. Damn her and her accusations. What did she know about it, anyway?

Cal drove home in an angry mood. He had gone to Catherine's today to force a confrontation, but had succeeded only in prolonging it.

THREE

The Pitchfork ranch was bounded on the west by the Rockies, on the north and east by Alberta's rich oil fields, and on the south by Angus Coleman's sheep ranch.

Once comprising a quarter of a million acres of land, its roots sank deep into the soil of Canadian history. The first seeds were planted toward the middle of the nineteenth century when the buffalo began to disappear from the American plains, and Americans began driving in small herds of cattle up from Montana. The Northwest Mounted Police had provided the security needed for open grazing and gave the new ranchers a small but steady market for their beef. As officers of the NWMP retired, they joined the ranching fraternity. Henry Walker, Cal's grandfather, had been among them, and Pitchfork was born. Years later, Cal's father expanded the thriving cattle ranch by building one of the largest integrated meat-packing businesses in the province of Alberta.

Things were different now, however. The cooks, the gardeners, and the maids had all disappeared. Nowadays, Pitchfork sat on forty thousand acres of private and leased land, employing a handful of cowboys instead of a hundred, and a single housekeeper rather than a staff of servants.

Catherine was quick to notice the changes as she wandered about the grounds sipping from a cold can of beer. None of the faces around her were recognizable, and yet so much else seemed familiar. The aroma of succulent ribs roasting over the open pit, for instance. The crackle of fat hitting red-hot coals. The ice-filled barrels of beer cooling in the shade beneath the trees. Every smell, taste, and sound combined to erase the years and plunge her back to a happier time, when the Pitchfork barbecue was the event of the summer season. She looked around, shaking her head, wondering how was it possible for so much to change and yet remain the same.

"Can I get you another one of those?"

Catherine looked up from her thoughts of long ago at the man who had spoken, and smiled. "No, thanks, I'm still working on this one."

He reached into a nearby barrel and pulled out a can of beer for himself. Popping the top he said, "My name is Drew Devlin." He offered a cold, wet hand.

"How do you do," she said. "I'm Catherine Coleman."

"Yes, I know."

She arched a questioning brow at him, to which he explained, "News travels fast in these parts."

"Are you any relation to Doctor Devlin, the veterinarian from Leduc? I understand he's in Edmonton now."

"He was my uncle."

"Was?"

"He's been dead for five years. I took over his practice. Moved in to Edmonton where the money is."

Catherine squinted her eyes to assess him in the bright daylight. She judged him to be in his mid-forties, a man obviously accustomed to fine things, if his style was any indication of it. He wore tailored jeans with a designer's name on the waistband. The familiar logo of an alligator was stitched to the pocket of his polo shirt. She noticed that his hands were neatly manicured. On the pinky of his right hand he wore an expensive gold ring set with diamonds around a blue star sapphire. An equally costly gold watch adorned his left wrist.

Catherine had never cared for ostentatious displays of wealth so, in spite of his friendliness, she felt an almost instant dislike for the man. She couldn't imagine a man like this wading ankle deep in hay tending to barn animals, or skirting cow-chips out in the open pasture.

"I'm surprised to see anyone from the Coleman place at Pitchfork today," he said, "or any day for that matter."

"And why is that?" she asked.

"It's pretty well known in these parts that the Colemans and the Walkers were never the best of friends."

The feud that had existed for years between the Colemans and the Walkers was often the subject of local gossip. No doubt her own reckless friendship with Cal had raised some eyebrows.

She gave the inquisitive veterinarian a noncommittal shrug, and said, "You know how it is. Cattle and sheep mix about as well as oil and water." With that, she bid him a good day and walked off.

On her own again, Catherine strolled the grounds, smiling and chatting with the other guests, pretending a lightheartedness she did not feel. Inwardly, she was regretting the foolishness of having come here today. There were too many memories lurking among these dusty corrals and footpaths. Too much remembering in spite of herself. She dared not venture too close to the house itself, for there was no telling what remembrances awaited there . . . especially there. She could not, however, stop herself from turning to look at it.

A shudder of recognition went through her at the sight of the big old house made of timber and stone. It had been built by Cal's grandfather with room in mind for the children and grandchildren to come. The generations, however, had produced only one son and one grandson, leaving many of the rooms to remain empty, with white spreads of cloth shrouding the furnishings.

Catherine and Cal used to play hide-and-seek in those abandoned rooms. They were terrified to be among the ghostly furnishings, of course, but they were young and possessed all the eagerness for life that overrides the fear of it.

Later on, when they were no longer so young, they discovered something else besides bravery in those gloomy, deserted rooms. They discovered each other. She remembered how close they had come at times, how lost in each other they would become before sanity restrained them in the nick of time. She could still hear Cal's soft curses between deep breaths, and recall her own spiral back to earth with a mixture of relief and regret. They had never achieved that one final act of intimacy, mutually resolving to save it for the day they were wed, never suspecting that such a day would never come.

Cal stood apart, watching the crowd with disinterest. Neighbors and acquaintances had come from miles around to be here this afternoon. Despite the good turnout, however, Cal was neither impressed nor flattered. It wasn't him they came to see each year. It was Walker beef that drew them—not just the ribs roasting in the open pit, but that which fed the entire province.

In the midst of his thoughts, Cal looked up and saw Catherine in the distance. He was mesmerized by the way she moved, with long, easy strides, exuding a kind of unaffected sexiness that made his throat go dry. His attention fixed on the way she lifted the can of beer to her lips, the slender column of her throat as she drank, the unconscious sweep of her hand across her bare neck to brush away the strands of dark hair that had escaped from the loose knot atop her head.

She was wearing a sundress of white linen with thin straps and eyelet lace at the hem. Simple silver hoops dangled from her earlobes. Around one wrist was clasped a sterling cuff. On her, simplicity was stunning, and Cal was powerless to ignore it. It lured him toward her in spite of his determination to keep his distance.

"I see you made it." *Brilliant, Walker,* he thought

disgustedly as soon as the words slipped out. Of course, she made it or she wouldn't be here. It was, he knew, the closeness of her that made him say stupid things. He warned himself to be careful.

Catherine turned to the sound of his voice. "Hello, Cal."

"Can I get you another one of those?"

Without waiting for a response, he took the can from her hand and tossed it into the trash. Reaching into the ice-filled barrel he pulled out another. His touch was cold and wet when he handed the can to Catherine, but the impact was no less heated than if he had plunged his hand into fire. They were both jarred by the effect of it.

He looked past her toward the house and said, "I put a new roof on a couple of years ago and fixed it up a little inside. It's always been too big for me, but . . ." He shrugged. ". . . it's home." Turning back to her, he spread his arms wide, gesturing around them, and ventured, "So? What do you think?"

"Lots of new faces," she replied. "But the place still looks the same."

"For the most part, it is. I made a few changes when I took over. Mainly, I just trimmed the luxuries. It was a matter of staying in business or not."

She looked about. The white fences were neat and trim. The grounds were well maintained. The cattle she had seen grazing in the pastures when driving in were fat and healthy. Cal obviously knew what he was doing. She wasn't surprised. Ranching had always been in his blood. She could just picture him bounding around the ranch in his pickup, mending fences, vaccinating the cattle, de-horning the bulls.

The picture it evoked of a hardworking, energetic man was not without its appeal.

Cal lifted the can to his mouth and took several long swallows of frosty beer. He ran his tongue across his lips in a movement that was both natural and relaxed in spite of his caution.

"On other spreads one person does one job," he explained, "but here on Pitchfork, whatever the job is—calving, farming, irrigating, plumbing—everyone knows how to do it. I hire the best people I can find. My rule is a simple one. I treat my employees with respect and I pay them well."

"It looks like you're thriving."

"We do all right. After my father died, the place floundered for a while until I returned and got it back on its feet. The first few years were rough. I worked from dawn to dusk alongside the hired hands. I figure, if you're going to tell someone to do something, you ought to show him that you're not afraid to do it yourself. At night I worked planning new projects and taking care of the paperwork. Some of it was luck, but mostly it was hard work."

He remembered the back-breaking labor that had seemed so necessary, not just to get the ranch going again, but to escape from the agonizing memory of Cathy. His changeable eyes swept the surroundings. With a slow nod of the head, he concluded, "Yeah, we do all right."

Pitchfork had always been a special place to Cal. Catherine noticed that even now, just talking about it, seemed to temper his hostility toward her. She took advantage of the opportunity to probe a little deeper. "What did you do when you left Pitchfork?"

He took the question in stride, as if he'd been

expecting it all along. "I did some wildcatting up north. Knocked around for a few years. I came back when my father died. I just couldn't let the place die with him."

Catherine was tempted to use his unusual easy mood to ask more questions. Like why he left Pitchfork. What made him stay away for so long? And where did he get that scar on his face? But not wishing to provoke his anger, she steered the conversation in another direction by asking, "Do you use Drew Devlin?"

"No. I've got my own vet here at Pitchfork."

"Is Devlin a friend of yours?"

"Hardly."

"Then why did you invite him here today?"

"I didn't. Millie did. Millie's the housekeeper. These get-togethers don't interest me anymore, at least not since—" He caught himself in the nick of time, just as he'd been about to say, at least not since you left, but he made a smooth transition. "If it were up to me, I'd call the whole thing off, but since it's become such a tradition, I let Millie invite whoever she wants. Why do you ask about Devlin?"

"I was considering using him, but I'm not sure. There's something about him that bothers me. He's so flashy."

"That doesn't mean he's not a good vet. Who are you currently using?"

"Ben's been using a vet in Leduc."

"No wonder you're thinking of switching vets," Cal said disparagingly. "You might also consider switching your foreman."

"What have you got against Ben?" she asked.

"The guy just rubs me the wrong way."

"In some ways he's a lot like you," said Catherine. "You're both irrascible and opinionated. Maybe that's what you don't like about him. And for your information, Ben has nothing to do with my reasons for switching vets. It's just that—" She stopped, realizing that she had said more than she wanted to.

"It's just that what?"

She was reluctant to tell him about the dead sheep she and Ben had found yesterday while looking for strays. "I hear he's very good, and he's closer than Leduc."

"Hey, Cathy, you don't have to rationalize to me. You want to use him, use him. Besides, I know that vet in Leduc, and Devlin is better. If I didn't keep a fulltime vet on staff, I'd probably use him myself."

His endorsement failed to buoy her. This thing with the sheep was upsetting her more than she cared to admit.

Cal saw the worried look that shadowed her features and said on impulse. "Come on, let's get out of here." Instinctively, his hand reached out for hers.

Catherine held back. "You mean leave?"

"Why not?"

"What would the others think?"

Cal's laugh had an abrasive edge. "Since when did you ever care what others think?"

It was easier to blame it on others than to blame it on herself, of course. The truth was, she was afraid to be alone with him. Yet while a heated inner voice warned her not to go, the words that formed on her tongue had an entirely different sound. "All right, sure. Why not?" It took every bit of willpower she had, however, to ignore the outstretched hand, whose strong brown fingers beckoned to her as if it had been yesterday.

Cal dropped his hand to his side, shrugged with feigned indifference, and led the way to his pickup, which was parked in the gravel driveway behind the house. If she wanted to be that way, fine, he thought. Without bothering to open the door for her, he started up the engine and drove away with a peel of the tires.

They drove with the windows rolled down and the summer breeze whipping past their faces. The air grew noticeably cooler the higher they drove into the hills. The sounds of civilization could not penetrate the dense curtain of wilderness that surrounded them. Not even the sound of their voices broke the perfect stillness as they drove in silence.

There was a calm up here, a solitude that Catherine had always found strangely comforting. The sky was blue and clear and so big that everything else looked dwarfed in comparison.

Cal drove with his hand relaxed on the wheel as if he had no particular destination in mind, but Catherine knew where he was taking her. Resigned to the fact that there was no place they could go that would not stir up the past like a hornet's nest, she sat back and watched the scenery pass by the window.

When they got to where they were going, Cal parked the pickup and turned off the engine. A tremor of recognition raced through Catherine as she climbed down from the cab and walked with Cal to the edge of the clearing. There, about a hundred yards from where they stood, was a sloping precipice that opened up the panorama for miles in every direction. The beauty of it staggered Catherine almost as much as the memory of these hills, one rolling over the other into infinity. From this spot, the echoes she and Cal used to shout into the air went on seemingly forever. Back then, it had been the most natural thing in the world for her to cup her hands to her mouth and shout, "I love you, Calvin Walker!" into the air and hear the echo of her words boomerang back to them.

Cal's deep voice at her side only strengthened the recollection. "It's not exactly the end of the world," he said, "but you can almost see it from here."

She smiled in spite of herself. "I used to love the way the sun set right over there." She stretched a bare arm toward a familiar spot on the western horizon. Unbidden, she confessed, "The city is okay, but it doesn't have sunsets like the ones up here." She was referring, he knew, to Boston, where she had lived as a child with her parents and later with her husband.

"Does it have shooting galleries?" he quipped.

She looked at him quizzically.

"I notice you haven't lost your skill with a rifle. I thought maybe you'd been practicing all these years."

The reminder of the shot she'd fired at him from the hillside made Catherine blush. Sheepishly, she said, "I guess there are just some things you never forget how to do. Like riding a bicycle."

Cal was disarmed by the dose of humor accompanied by an impish flash from her dark eyes. She was utterly beautiful and utterly believable. To him, an utterly unfair combination.

There had gnawed at Cal all these years an intolerable desire each time he'd thought of her. He used to think if only she was here . . . And yet here she was now, an arm's length away, and just as inaccessible. Something churned inside of him. Seeing her again like this was perhaps the worst and sweetest torture he would ever know.

He cleared his throat and said, "I thought you might have gotten a little rusty, that's all."

"Even if I have, I'll bet I can still outshoot you."

He was almost as amused by her arrogance as he was annoyed by it. "Oh, yeah?"

"Yeah."

He pivoted on his boot heels and strode back to the pickup. Reaching behind the front seat he pulled out his rifle and returned with it to where she was standing. He lifted the weapon to his shoulder, bracing the hilt against the taut muscle. Squinting into the viewfinder, he scanned the area for a suitable target. "That tree that cuts at an angle," he said of a pine in the distance that had been split by lightning. Taking careful aim, he fired. He lowered the rifle and thrust it out to Catherine, challenging, "Prove it."

Catherine took the rifle and positioned it at her shoulder. Sighting the target, she held it in view as her finger tightened on the trigger. The sound of her gunshot cracked the air like thunder. Lowering the rifle, she handed it back to Cal. "Shall we go have a look?"

They started down the hill toward the split pine. When they got there, an examination of the trunk revealed a single bullet hole.

Cal was confident that his bullet had hit its mark because when he fired, he'd seen a bit of bark fly off the tree through the viewfinder. He took a pen knife from his back pocket and began to dig it out. Chips of bark flew into the air as he worked. Suddenly, the metal tip of the knife struck something metallic. He dug a little more and pulled out a spent shell, exclaiming triumphantly, "Aha!"

"Let me see that." She grabbed it away from him and examined it. There was no question but that the shell had been recently fired. Rolling it around her palm she muttered, "I don't know."

Cal protested. "Are you telling me I didn't hit that tree?"

"Not at all."

"Are you saying that the shell in your palm didn't come from my rifle?"

"Of course not."

He concluded with typical arrogance, "Then it's my bullet."

"If you mean it's your bullet because it came from your rifle, you're right," she said. "But if you mean that it's your bullet because you fired it, I'm afraid you're wrong." She pointed at the pen knife. "May I have that for a moment, please?"

He gave it to her grudgingly.

Catherine went to the tree and began to dig in the same hole from which Cal had extracted the bullet. "You see, Cal," she said as she worked, "that bullet you just dug out of this tree was fired from your rifle, but it wasn't fired by you." She stopped digging and turned back to him. "*This* is the bullet you fired."

Between her thumb and forefinger she held the projectile she had just dug out of the tree. "You did hit the tree. But so did I. Your bullet went in first. Mine went in after yours."

Cal looked from the small black hole in the bark

to the two spent shells in Catherine's palm and back again to the tree before realizing he'd lost the contest. The air went out of him in a whoosh. He was stunned. She had aimed not just for the tree, but for his own bullet hole, and had hit it! With the possible exception of Annie Oakley, who but Cathy could pull off a stunt like that? He was torn at first between indignation and foolishness. And then he began to laugh.

Catherine's adrenaline was running high in the aftermath of the shooting contest. It amazed her that the simple act of aiming a rifle at a tree and pulling the trigger could excite her as much as it did, certainly more than anything she could remember in a long time. But it was more than that which moved her in this way, and she knew it. With the exception of the scar on Cal's face, for a few brief moments he reminded Catherine of the Cal of old. It was the manner in which he had challenged her, with that streak of arrogance that was so much a part of him. It was the way he accepted losing, without hard feelings or wounded pride, but with genuine good humor and the ability to laugh at himself. It was the way he looked at this moment, strong and relaxed. It was the way he smelled. It was simply and purely, him.

"Angus would be proud," he said appreciatingly. "He loved to watch you out-shoot everyone else."

The familiarity of his tone beckoned unwelcome memories in Catherine of the man she used to know. It took all her willpower to remind herself that the face smiling at her, with its strangely scarred handsomeness, did not belong to the man she remembered.

Catherine was not the only one bothered by memories.

"Yeah," said Cal, "that Angus, I loved that old man."

"A lot of people did. There was quite a turnout at his funeral."

"I know. I was there." In answer to the surprise that registered on her face he added, "I went to pay my respects. It had nothing to do with you and me, so I thought it best to keep my presence to myself."

The day of the funeral Catherine had searched the faces in the crowd for a glimpse of Cal, but he'd been conspicuously absent. Or so she thought until now. In spite of the pinpricks of pain she was feeling at this moment at having had him so close that day and not knowing it, she admitted truthfully, "Angus would have wanted you there."

And you? Cal was thinking. Would you have wanted me there if you had known?

He remembered that day as if it were yesterday. A hot, dusty, grief-filled day in late August, the mourners gathered around the grave, Catherine looking tired and withdrawn beneath a black veil. How he had wanted to go to her. It had been the hardest thing he'd ever done, to just stand there in the distance watching her. Too much foolish pride had prevented him from going to her that day. He wanted to go to her still, but these days it was a hard-bitten, stiff-necked emotion that gave Cal a slightly tougher edge, strengthening his resolve to resist her.

"My father used to rant and rave about the way Angus's sheep were eating up the pastures," Cal reflected. "But I'll bet that if he'd been alive at the time, he'd have been at the funeral."

Catherine seized upon the remark. "What difference did it make to your father if Angus's sheep were eating up the pastureland? They were Angus's pastures, weren't they?"

Cal responded with equal speed at the question, which he knew was not a question at all but an accusation. "Some of that was leased land," he asserted. "Our grandfathers signed a joint lease for it back in the thirties."

"I know that. It seems the only one who didn't know it was your father."

"What's that supposed to mean?"

"Come on, Cal. I used to hear my grandfather complain all the time about the way your father used to run our sheep off that leased land. Which raises the question of why your father was chasing sheep off land leased jointly with a sheep rancher."

Cal's stance stiffened. "What are you suggesting?"

"I'm not suggesting anything. All I'm saying is that my grandfather had his problems with the Walkers, and so do I."

"I hope you're not going to accuse me of running your sheep off that land."

Catherine searched her mind for some infraction, no matter how slight, to hold against him. Recalling Ben's story, she complained, "You gave my foreman a hard time about the fence in the north pasture."

"It was on my land," he insisted.

"Isn't that just like a Walker? All that land and still it's not enough."

"Not enough?" he echoed. "You ought to know, Cathy. Aren't you the one who wanted more than a mere cattle rancher could give you?"

The remark was meant to sting, and it did.

"Is that what you think?"

"What am I supposed to think?" he shot back defensively. "What is it your ex-husband does for a living? Yeah, I'd say a real-estate tycoon and—what is it the newspapers call him?—senatorial hopeful was able to give the daughter of Ellis Randolph a hell of a lot more than a cattle rancher from the middle of nowhere."

The few brief moments of ease between them shattered like glass. Catherine reproached herself for not knowing that it would come to this. She turned away and started back up the hill.

Cal followed her. "I read in the newspaper that you didn't take anything from the guy when you left him."

The climb was steeper than it looked. The lean muscles in Catherine's legs were working hard and her lungs were drawing in air deeply. In a breathless voice she said, "I left that marriage with exactly what I brought into it—me."

"What about your inheritance?" he asked behind her. "Your father must have left you a tidy sum."

From over her shoulder she responded bitterly, "Divorce lawyers are expensive. There's nothing left."

"No alimony?"

"I refused it."

"Well, I think you made a mistake," said Cal. "From the look of things, you need all the money you can get to keep your ranch going."

She could tell by the tone of his voice that he was mocking her. "If I'm making a mistake, it's my business. Besides, it wouldn't be the biggest mistake I've ever made."

"You're right. The biggest mistake you ever made was marrying the guy in the first place."

Catherine halted in her tracks and whirled to face him. Furiously, she said, "That's presumptuous!"

"You don't have to admit it if you don't want to, Cathy, but at least spare me the insult of denying it."

It was like waving a red flag at her. She opened her mouth to respond, but got no further than drawing in her breath. She knew she had stepped on the loose stones only when it was too late. They rolled like marbles beneath her sandal, throwing her off balance on the already precarious hillside. She gave a small cry as her arms flew out to her sides. If Cal hadn't been there, she would have toppled all the way down the steep hill for sure. As it was, she fell backwards into his arms, hard up against his chest.

The breath went out of Cal on contact. Despite two small steps backward his strength prevailed, keeping them both on their feet.

It took only seconds for it to happen, far too fast for Catherine to prepare herself for the dizzy feeling of being in his arms. She knew instantly that no matter how many bumps and bruises she would have suffered tumbling down the hill, she was in far greater danger now.

Afterwards, there would be time to remember and to reproach herself for the way she responded. For now, there was only the dim awareness of turning in his embrace. All logic drowned in a sea of emotion as her arms came up around his neck. For many wordless moments they stood like that looking into each other's eyes, each apprehensive about what would happen next if they let it. In the hazy green depths of Cal's eyes, Catherine recognized a welcome-home look. Something inside of her melted at the sight of it.

His kiss was soft and tentative at first. His lips moved over hers with a natural curiosity, recalling the texture and taste of her. What was it she had said earlier? There are some things you never forget. God, she was right. The aching familiarity only deepened Cal's intent. He kissed her harder, hungrily making up for lost time.

Her own soft, wet tongue met his halfway in a rediscovery that left them both breathless. Her head fell back against the rake of his mouth along the smooth column of her throat, at her ear, over her cheek.

For a few brief moments, it was as if nothing had changed. She was eighteen again and desperately in love. She remembered it all—the heat of his palm against her flesh, the fire of his lips igniting hers, the sound of his raspy breath at her ear, the swelling of his body against hers. She was certain that if she opened her eyes, everything that had happened between then and now would have vanished.

Her body moved instinctively against his the way it used to. The blood pounded at her temples in a familiar frantic rhythm. She was too caught up in remembering to think about where they were headed.

When Catherine finally did open her eyes, she realized with a start just how foolish she was to think that nothing had changed. The sight of that scar set amidst familiar features made her pull back. This time she recalled the rest of it, not just the passion but the pain as well, every bit of it, and all such a long time ago. Something rebelled inside of her at the weakness that made it impossible to resist him. How could she have let it happen? she thought, aghast. Was she out of her mind? Riddled with shame at the ease with which she had succumbed to her own desire, she pushed herself away from him.

Cal was as surprised by his own actions as Catherine was by hers, but it felt so good to hold her that for a moment he'd forgotten everything else. There was an expression of hurt bewilderment on his face as he reached out a hand to her. "Cathy?"

But she was already running back up the hill.

The pent-up passion, the momentary thrill, the disappointment tearing through him, all worked to fire up Cal's fury.

"Cathy!"

He shouted her name and heard the sound of his own anger and pain resound off the hills in a series of echoes that seemed to go on forever.

FOUR

How things had changed. The city had grown, first as an administrative center for the province as its capital, then for the petroleum industry. It was hard to imagine that this clean, vibrant, and young city of a half-million people had once been a town of fur traders, trappers, Indians, and missionaries, and had served as a backdoor to the Klondike goldfields.

Catherine's first memories of Edmonton were of the construction cranes that had been everywhere. Back then, it was one of the fastest growing cities in Canada, made so by the massive exploitation of Alberta's crude-oil reserves spurred on by the world energy crisis.

She remembered the stories her grandfather used to tell of the thousands of fortune seekers who left Edmonton for the Klondike, and how only about one-quarter of them actually made it to the gold fields, fewer still prospering when they got there. Best of all, she liked the stories he told about how he and some of his pioneering bush pilot buddies, all World War I flying aces to boot, made aviation history by linking Edmonton by air with the far north, making Edmonton the gateway to the Arctic.

Catherine had her mother to thank for being allowed to stay with her grandparents during the summers. Ellis Randolph hadn't thought it an appropriate place for Catherine to be, complaining that his daughter was wild enough on her own without running around in the wilds of the Canadian Rockies. Mary Randolph, however, had different ideas. Having grown up in the foothills, she was determined to nurture the very wildness her husband eschewed in Catherine by sending the girl north each summer.

With the exception of that one year when her grandmother died, Catherine's summers had been happy ones. Those last few in particular, when she and the son of the neighboring cattle rancher had discovered each other, would linger always in Catherine's memory. It wasn't possible to forget that kind of passion, made all the more memorable by never having reached its fullest potential. Nor forget the promises they had uttered, made all the more painful when broken.

When Catherine pulled into the office complex parking lot, a sign instructing clients to park in the rear for pick-ups and deliveries led her around back, where she pulled into the space beside a late-model van with dark-tinted windows. She didn't get out of the car right away. She hadn't been inside a veterinarian's office since the last time Angus had sent her to Doc Devlin's for supplies. She remembered it as if it had been yesterday.

It had been shortly before she left Alberta, supposedly for good. They'd had words just that morning over, of all things, Cal Walker. Angus just couldn't believe that Cal was gone for good. *Refused* to believe it, damn him, despite all indications to the contrary.

She had railed that day at that stubborn streak in his Scottish soul. The very tenacity she inherited from him, which was at times a blessing, at times a curse, turned out to be a curse that day. She was still reeling from the shock of Cal's leaving to have much patience with her grandfather's behavior. Why couldn't he just accept that Cal was gone for good, instead of arguing that it didn't make any sense, that Cal wouldn't just go off like that without a good reason? He'd even gone so far as to defend Cal—as if there could be a reason for betrayal or a defense against its pain.

Shortly after her argument with Angus, Catherine left Canada. By then there were no hard feelings left between them—she'd never been able to stay angry with him for very long, anyway. And that, as they say, was that.

Business must be good, thought Catherine when she entered the plushly-carpeted waiting room and looked around. It was doubtful, of course, that a veterinarian could ever earn in ten years the kind of money that men like her father and ex-husband earned in a single year, yet it was also equally obvious from the look of things that this was one resourceful veterinarian.

The old oak furnishings that Catherine remembered from Doc Devlin's office, with their patina of age and smell of linseed oil, were gone, replaced by the sleek black matte of high-tech design. The worn copies of *Readers' Digest* and *Ladies Home Journal* were missing, as well. In their place she saw news weeklies and veterinary journals. There was a distinct absence of familiar animal smells permeating the air, only the sweet, faintly cloying scent of the perfume worn by the receptionist who took Catherine's name and told her to be seated.

From the financial journals that were meticulously arranged on the glass-top end table, Catherine concluded that the younger Doctor Devlin must have a genius for the stock market, or else some lucky speculations had paid off. Surely, his veterinary practice alone couldn't account for what she saw around her, although even she was forced to admit that his credentials were impressive.

Encased behind glass in an expensive frame on the wall was a hand-lettered diploma on ivory parchment from Cornell University, certifying Drew Devlin as a Doctor of Veterinary Medicine. Other testimonials from Canadian and American veterinary medical associations, similarly framed, were hung about the wood-paneled walls of the waiting room.

No mention of fees had been made when Catherine had phoned him earlier that morning. She had obtained his assurance that he could see her without an appointment, and she promptly drove to Edmonton. Looking back, she realized she should have guessed that afternoon at Pitchfork that his fees would be high. What she saw around her now only confirmed it. She wondered if that was his Jaguar she'd seen parked outside in the space marked private. Was the van parked in the back his also? Catherine wouldn't have been at all surprised if it was.

To his credit, he did not keep her waiting long.

"Thank you again for seeing me without an appointment," Catherine told him as he escorted her inside.

"Not at all," Devlin replied. "I was hoping you'd come by."

As she walked with him down a tiled corridor to his office, she got glimpses of several of the examining rooms. All were tastefully appointed, no doubt to impress the pet owners who were shelling out hefty sums of cash for his services.

He motioned for Catherine to have a seat on the black leather sofa. He took the matching leather armchair opposite her.

"I didn't get a chance on Sunday to ask you how you like being back," he said.

"To tell the truth," replied Catherine, "I've been working so much lately I haven't had the time to think about it." Then, with a ring of self-mockery in her tone, "I guess I can forget about all those aerobics classes I went to in Boston. All the aerobics workouts in the world couldn't have prepared me for the kind of work I've been doing lately. I've discovered muscles I never knew existed."

He nodded as if he understood. "Maybe you'd be better off selling the place," he suggested. "While you can still get something for it."

Catherine didn't care for his presumption that the place meant so little to her that she would consider selling it. But she hadn't come here today to defend herself or to justify her actions to anyone; she'd come here on business. So, despite the nagging reservation she had about him in the back of her mind, Catherine refrained from setting him straight. After all, he was supposed to be the best there was, and right now, that's what she needed.

"I'd be hard pressed to get much for it at the moment," she said.

"If that's the case," said Devlin, "I'd sell if I were you."

Well, you're not *me,* Catherine thought mutinously.

"I'm sure you're right," she said. "But it seems I've inherited more than a sheep ranch from my grandfather. I seem to have inherited his stubbornness, as well. I'm determined to make a business out of that place if it kills me."

"Let's hope it doesn't get to that point," Devlin said with a laugh. "And besides, you wouldn't want to leave your heirs with a bankrupt sheep ranch on their hands."

"No problem there," said Catherine.

"How's that?"

"No heirs."

"No one?"

"Just me."

"No children?"

She had tried without success to have a child during the early years of her marriage, foolishly thinking a child might help fill the space left by a husband who was married more to his business than to her. In retrospect, she supposed she was lucky that no children had been born of a union doomed to failure from the start. The divorce had been bitter enough on its own without dragging innocent children through it.

"Just me," she repeated. The frosty edge to her voice told Devlin that he had taken entirely too much for granted by probing into a private corner of her life. They hardly knew each other, after all, and Catherine was not accustomed to sharing such deeply-held thoughts with strangers.

Noting her sudden withdrawal, Devlin held up his left hand and wiggled his fingers to emphasize the absence of a gold band. "I'm a bachelor myself, so I guess that puts us in the same category."

The possibility of having anything in common with him was remote, Catherine thought dryly.

"The city certainly has changed a lot in the last ten years," she said, adroitly changing the subject. "I hardly recognized it when I drove in."

"I know what you mean. First the boom, then the glut. Natural gas is the thing now."

"Maybe so. I'm sure a big old gusher would make a lot of people just as happy, though," said Catherine, thinking fatalistically that it would certainly help her own bleak situation.

"Yes," he agreed, "it would. It's too bad you don't have any rigs going on your land, Catherine. From what I hear, you could use it."

His continued reference to the sorry state of the ranch was beginning to grate on Catherine's nerves. She met his gaze with her own dark and steady one. "Have you been out there lately to see for yourself, doctor?"

The directness of her question caught him by surprise. "Why, no, I haven't. One, well, one hears things."

"I see. And what sort of things have you heard?" Her dark eyes gazed at him forthrightly without wavering, almost as if daring him to answer.

"Everyone pretty much knows that the place has gone downhill since Angus died. There's talk that you've lost some of your sheep. And then, of course, it can't be easy for you being around Cal Walker, seeing as how—'' His words trailed off into an awkward but telling silence.

Catherine felt an unwanted quickening of her pulse at the mention of Cal's name, followed by a rapid rising of her anger. *That* was one subject she would not discuss with him. She wasn't surprised that he knew about her and Cal. He probably heard about it from his uncle, who'd been not only Angus' veterinarian but an old friend as well. No, what surprised and angered Catherine most was that he knew about the dead sheep.

Because of the avalanche of publicity her divorce had generated, Catherine had come to guard her privacy fiercely. She didn't like the idea that Devlin, or anyone else for that matter, knew her business, especially since she knew damned well that she was being judged by them all. By Drew Devlin with his flamboyant airs. By Ben McFarland with his mounting resentment. And by Cal Walker with those damnable green eyes, which had the ability to turn dark, almost brown, and burn holes clear to her soul.

She shook herself loose from the memory of those eyes, and said, ''You haven't asked me why I'm here.''

Devlin smiled. He purposely hadn't asked, waiting instead for her to bring it up and, in seeking his help, establish her need of him. ''As much as I'd like to think it was for the conversation,'' he said, still smiling, ''something tells me otherwise.''

''It's business.''

''Frankly, I was hoping it would be. I've been after your business for years.''

"I think you're being modest," said Catherine. "You appear to be doing very well without my business."

"Nevertheless, your grandfather and my uncle did business together, why shouldn't we? So, what can I do for you?"

"You can take a look at the carcass I brought."

"You've brought a carcass?" He moved forward a little in his seat, seeming interested. "Where is it?"

"It's out back in the station wagon."

"What? In this heat?" His reaction was swift and genuine as he sprang to his feet and strode to the door. When she started after him, he put his hand up to halt her. "No, no, Catherine, you wait for me here."

She bristled at his tone of voice because she got the distinct impression that she was being dismissed. Nevertheless, his departure gave Catherine a chance to catch the breath that had lodged in her throat at the unexpected mention of Cal's name. Despite the struggle she was waging to maintain a level expression and a smooth voice, she was still hurling reproaches at herself even now, days later, for having gone to Pitchfork on Sunday. The onslaught of memories, followed by the assault of Cal's kiss, had Catherine's temperature hovering somewhere above normal. It tinted her cheeks with a perpetual flush that was easy enough to blame on the August heat. She only hoped that Drew Devlin hadn't noticed the slight flutter of her breath at the mention of Cal's name.

Catherine glanced at her watch. It was getting late. It would be dark in a couple of hours. She felt a sudden need to be on her way, to be back home in the foothills.

She couldn't be sure how much coverage, if any, her divorce had gotten in the Edmonton papers. The chance of being recognized had made Catherine gun-shy of densely-populated areas. She had come to crave anonymity and the freedom it afforded to be able to walk down the street without attracting stares. She'd been tempted to send Ben to Edmonton with the carcass, but then she reminded herself that this was Edmonton, not Boston, Massachusetts, where she'd spent the past ten years of her life. It wasn't likely anyone here would know her or care.

But it was more than the possibility of being recognized that made Catherine anxious to return home. The city—Edmonton, Boston, any city—made her uncomfortable. Angus used to tease her, calling her a country girl at heart and telling her that she would always feel more comfortable with the rich Canadian soil beneath her feet than the hard city pavement.

Where was Devlin? she thought impatiently. What was keeping him?

Just then the door opened and he entered the office, wiping his wet hands on a paper towel. "You did a good job of transporting it," he said. "In this heat it's a good thing you thought to use ice."

She could tell that he was impressed, and it annoyed her. What did he take her for, a novice? She didn't need a diploma from Cornell University to know her way around a sheep ranch. With the possible exception of moving heavy equipment and hoisting objects that weighed twice as much as she did herself, there wasn't a job on the ranch she couldn't do.

From Angus she had learned how to assist the ewes during the birthing season and geld a rambunctious ram. There wasn't a fence she couldn't mend, a horse she couldn't ride, and a gun she couldn't shoot. And she damned well knew how to pack a carcass in ice.

The color rose to Catherine's cheeks from the temper that flared up inside of her. Nevertheless, her voice remained smooth and unaffected when she said, "It seemed the logical thing to do."

"I'll examine it later and let you know what I think," said Devlin.

"Oh. But I thought—" Surely, in the fifteen minutes he'd been gone, he had examined the carcass. But perhaps not. "Well, thank you, Doctor Devlin," she said, extending her hand to him.

"Please, call me Drew. Doctor Devlin is much too formal. And besides, it's almost like we know each other. After all—"

"I know," she interjected. "Your uncle and my grandfather."

"Precisely." His handshake had a soft, cool, unformidable feel to it.

She removed her hand from his and said with a confidence he found both surprising and excrutiating, "You'll find no discernible marks on the carcass. No outward indication of what it died of. I'd like you to do an autopsy."

She was obviously much more knowledgeable than he'd given her credit for being. And considerably more outspoken. He could see now that he had underestimated both her tenacity and her intelligence. "An autopsy," he repeated thoughtfully as he steered her toward the door. "Of course. I'll call you in a few days with the results."

She knew he hadn't expected her to know as much

as she did, and felt a small surge of triumph at his reaction. "Have your receptionist send me the bill."

"Now, Catherine, don't worry about that."

"Doctor Dev—Drew," she quickly corrected when he shook a finger at her, "I think it's safe to assume that you haven't attained all of this—" she gestured with wide arms around them, "—by not charging for your services."

"Hardly. Actually, my fees are quite high. I only meant that your credit here is good. After all—"

"Right," she said as she moved past him out the door, "Your uncle and my grandfather."

There was something about Drew Devlin that made Catherine uncomfortable, but it wasn't until she was driving home that she realized what it was. Just as she had that day at Pitchfork, she had sensed today his eagerness to please. Why? she wondered. He'd made no passes at her, so he couldn't be interested in her for personal reasons. She was thankful for that, for he was hardly her type. And it couldn't really be her business he was after when he appeared to be doing very nicely without her.

She thought about what he'd said about his uncle and her grandfather. Sure, Angus Coleman and Andrew Devlin had been friends for as long as she could remember, but was that really all that important to Drew Devlin? In all the summers she had spent at the ranch with her grandmother and grandfather, Catherine had not once run into Andrew Devlin's nephew Drew. When her grandmother died the summer Catherine turned fourteen, Andrew Devlin had been at the funeral, but she could not remember seeing this nephew who placed such emphasis on the friendship.

His subtle probing into her affairs annoyed her. Worse was his particular emphasis on the unfortunate run of bad luck that had befallen the ranch ever since her return. It was too bad Drew Devlin hadn't inherited any of his uncle's warmth and humor, Catherine complained to herself as she drove on into the night.

The thought of the ranch teetering on the brink of bankruptcy, and the persistent ache of missing Angus, sent Catherine's spirits into decline. She drew in a ragged breath and let it out slowly. She had no one to turn to, no one to trust, least of all the three men she'd come in contact with since her return.

It had become increasingly apparent to Catherine in the weeks since her return that her foreman, Ben McFarland, resented her being there. She hadn't come back because she didn't think he was doing a good enough job, though. He'd had the thankless task of running things alone for six years. It was just that she had nowhere else to go. The dusty little sheep ranch in the foothills of the Canadian Rockies, from which she'd fled ten years earlier, was all that was left. But, of course, she couldn't explain all that to Ben.

The fact was, she needed Ben. Where could she find another foreman willing to take on a crumbling sheep ranch? She dared not risk alienating him and provoking him to quit, so she tolerated his belligerence and his open resentment with tight-lipped control.

And then there was Cal. Damn him and his fiery kiss that had aroused in her the memory of the unstoppable passion she used to feel in his arms.

With unwanted clarity, Catherine recalled the kiss

on the hillside that had sucked the breath right out of her lungs. There had been no tenderness in him as his mouth had savaged hers, no gentleness in those arms that held her. Those first few desperate moments in which it seemed they had both lost their minds had given Catherine no choice but to want it as much as he seemed to. She hadn't forgotten the feel of him, hard and soft all at once, nor the strong, clean taste of him. She had simply underestimated the effect it would have on her.

Catherine did not know how it was possible to be taken with a kiss alone, to be laid open and made to feel as valuable as if she'd been laying naked beneath him, but that was how it had felt. In those few furious seconds she had wanted him—not just the taut muscles and the sheer masculine strength of him—but the inner strength which she knew was there also. She found herself wondering what it would be like to make love to him, and hating herself for the thought.

His kiss had drained her of her will for several precarious seconds until reality came to the rescue. And then all she felt was shame and the desperate urge to run away. They had driven back to Pitchfork in tense silence, but what was there to say?

Of the three, Catherine was reluctant to trust Cal most of all. He was the one who could do the most damage. Hadn't he already proved that?

It was easy to let her thoughts take over when cruising an easy seventy-five miles per hour on the highway, but once Catherine got off the exit ramp, the curves in the road leading back to the ranch forced her thoughts back to driving.

The radio in the station wagon was tuned to a country-western station. Randy Travis was singing about the hard-rock bottom of somebody's heart, and Catherine was humming along to the music when the curves came up unexpectedly before her headlights. Instinctively, her foot went to the brake pedal. She pumped lightly, confident that the car would respond, but nothing happened. She pumped the brakes again, this time a little more forcefully, although still unaware that anything was amiss.

Suddenly, the road took a dip while curving sharply to the left. Rather than slowing down, the car was gaining speed. Catherine jammed her foot down hard on the brake pedal. Nothing happened. The dark night was flying past the window, sending her into a state of alarm. Her hand grabbed the gearshift knob. At this speed, downshifting made little difference. Without brakes to slow it down, the car careened out of control.

Catherine screamed and threw her arms up in front of her face as the car flew through the black night straight across the road and onto the shoulder, where it bumped its way into a ditch and skidded to a halt.

The seatbelt that was slashed across her chest kept Catherine's body in place, but it could not prevent her head from pitching forward and hitting the steering wheel with a jolt that was hard enough to stun her.

Catherine was unaware of the darkness beyond the windows or the rakish angle of the car's headlights, oblivious to her own low moan. Her head swam with dizziness. A place at her forehead throbbed with pain. She reached up to touch the spot and felt the warm stickiness of fresh blood. For several minutes she just sat there, stunned.

A gradual awareness came over her of where she

was and what had just happened, and with it came the shuddering relief at finding herself still alive. She could be lying here unconscious, or worse. That she had survived was a miracle. That it had occurred after dark when few cars travelled this road was a stroke of pure luck. If another car had been coming in the opposite direction . . . Catherine trembled to think of what might have happened.

In the aftermath of her brush with death, as she sat there in the car on the side of the road feeling alone and afraid, Catherine was seized with a sense of relief when a beam of headlights appeared in the dark distance.

It wasn't until the vehicle approached and slowed and came to an eventual stop up ahead on the road that she felt the first traces of renewed fear. She realized suddenly that it could be anyone and hastily reached over her shoulder to lock the door.

She watched as a figure moved from the cab of a pickup truck and walked toward the spot where her car had gone off the road. It was no more than a shadow, really, against the darkness, that grew larger as it approached. Catherine swallowed hard as the figure moved into the light of her headlamps, then she gasped. What was *he* doing here?

Cal Walker's broad-shouldered frame filled up the beam of light. Catherine recognized the stance, his feet planted slightly apart, arms at his sides, looking deceptively casual to anyone who didn't know better. There was a scowl on his face as he came forward.

Catherine was no longer aware of the throb at her forehead, nor even of the accident that had caused it. A renewed fear sprang up within her, for instead of her life, it was now her emotions that were in danger.

FIVE

He was at the window. His face, separated by only inches from hers by the pane of glass, looked handsome and scarred, angry and confused all at once. His eyes were wide and bright. He was saying something to her, shouting, it seemed, as he beat against the glass with his fist.

Still dazed, Catherine reached over mechanically and pulled up the button on the door. No sooner was the door unlocked than he jerked it open.

"My God, Cathy, what happened? Are you all right? No, don't talk. Just sit still."

He reached inside and began to touch her, carefully squeezing and probing, checking for broken bones. "Are you in any pain? Does it hurt anywhere?"

In the darkness, he could see that her face was chalk-white, and could hear the unmistakable strain of her breathing as his fingers raced smoothly up and down the length of her arms and then her legs.

"How are your ribs? Does it hurt when I do this?"

He placed both hands around her midsection, starting at the point just below her breasts and gently but firmly moving downward. He drew back quickly when she gasped. ''What is it, did I hurt you?''

Catherine was mortified. Her reaction had nothing at all to do with pain or discomfort. She wanted to shout at him to keep his infernal hands off of her. Wasn't it embarrassing enough to be reduced to such shameful quivering? Couldn't he see what his touch alone was doing to her?

In a weakened voice she answered, ''N–no,'' and squirmed away from him. ''I'm fine, Cal. Really. My head, that's all. I must have hit it on something when the car went out of control.''

''Let me have a look at that.'' He grasped her chin in his fingers and turned her face toward him. With a feather-light touch, he brushed her dark hair away from her face, sweeping the remaining strands off her forehead with the tip of his thumb.

The darkness forced him to move closer to see the bruise at her temple. When he did, Catherine had no choice but to breathe in his scent. That strangely intoxicating aroma of good, clean perspiration and natural male ambrosia that had always had a subtle impact on her senses was just as difficult to ignore tonight, in spite of the circumstances.

His warm breath felt like fire against her cheek as he examined the cut at her temple and concluded, ''It doesn't look too bad.''

He let her hair fall through his fingers and moved back a little to look at her. For several long moments his eyes probed her face. Then, satisfied that she was really all right, he stood up, reached inside the car for her hand, and said, "C'mon, I'll drive you home."

"The car—" she began.

"You can send someone back for it in the morning."

"But—"

"You can't sit there all night," he said. Then, reading her apprehension like a book, he scoffed, "Don't worry, Cathy, all I'm offering you is a ride home."

It was close inside the cab of the pickup truck, far too close for Catherine's liking. Still shaken from her narrow escape on the road, the last thing she needed was Cal's brooding presence beside her. In spite of the immediate concern he had shown, she could feel his growing hostility as he started up the engine. She noticed that he hadn't even bothered to ask her what happened.

Catherine spoke up tentatively, testing her voice against the silence. "I suppose I'm lucky that you drove by."

"Yeah, I suppose you are." His tone was decidedly unfriendly.

If he was so sorry for it now, why had he even bothered to offer her a ride home? Catherine huffed to herself. She turned her face toward the window so as not to look at that obstinate profile etched against the darkness. *What's his problem?* she wondered. She was the one who just nearly got killed. She was the one who should have the attitude.

Cal drove with his eyes glued to the road, feeling guilty. He hadn't meant to be mean, but, hell, she'd scared him half to death. Who could have guessed when he'd started out for Edmonton this morning on business that by nightfall he would find Catherine along the side of the road, sitting in a nearly-overturned station wagon with all the doors locked? One look at her, with her complexion as white as a sheet, and he'd been overwhelmed by a long-forgotten protective impulse. She had looked so frightened, so unbearably vulnerable that he'd wanted to put his arms around her and hold her, the way he used to do when she came to him for comfort. Only a strident inner reminder that that was all a long time ago prevented him from acting on his impulse and making a total fool of himself. Besides, the woman sitting pale-faced and terrified behind the steering wheel wasn't the girl he remembered, no matter how much she may have looked the same, nor how strongly his body still reacted to her.

"Do you want to tell me what happened?"

Catherine turned her attention away from the window at the sound of his deep voice. She shrugged honestly and replied, "I don't know what happened. One minute I was driving and everything was fine, and all of a sudden I just lost control."

Cal glanced skeptically over at her. It wasn't like Catherine to just lose control. "Maybe you hit something in the road."

She shuddered when the memory of it rushed back to her. She recalled the mild cause for concern she'd felt as she'd gone into that curve too fast, followed by blinding panic as the car had failed to respond to her foot's demand on the brake pedal. "It was the brakes. I kept stepping on the brakes, but the car wouldn't stop."

"I don't like the sound of that," Cal said roughly.

"Tell me something, who takes care of the vehicles on the ranch?"

"There's only the station wagon and an old pickup truck."

"Yeah, but who takes care of them?"

Catherine knew that maintenance of all vehicles and equipment on the ranch was, of course, Ben McFarland's responsibility. "What are you suggesting?" she asked him. But she knew what Cal was driving at. He had already made his dislike of her foreman obvious.

"Suggesting? Nothing. But if I were you, Cathy, I'd have a talk with that foreman of yours."

Here was another arrogant man presuming to tell her what he would do if he were her. With this one, however, Catherine felt less inclined to hold her tongue. "Thanks for the advice, Cal, but you're *not* me."

"You got that right," he said.

"What's that supposed to mean?"

In an excruciatingly caustic tone Cal replied, "Let's just say that I wouldn't have done some of the things you've done."

Like what? she wanted to ask. Like losing control over a car with no brakes? Like marrying someone you don't love? Like being foolish enough to love someone like *you*? Catherine bit back the words that lay like bitter pills upon her tongue. What did any of it matter?

The air inside the confined cab of the pickup grew thicker with tension as it took the curves of the long, lonely road. Catherine lay her head back against the seat and turned her face toward the window again, falling silent.

Cal could feel the distance growing wider between them. Well, what did he expect when she'd made her dislike of him known the moment they'd seen each other again? He'd been a fool to ever think that they would be able to put their differences aside for even a little while. But after all, it wasn't as if they'd never been close.

It was, in fact, the very closeness they used to share which told Cal now just how much she was shaken up over the accident. He felt like a heel for having treated her harshly. He hazarded a look in her direction. The night wind was rushing past the open window, whipping her dark hair away from her face. With her head tilted back, the smooth white column of her throat looked like marble in the moonlight. He knew from experience just how soft and silky it really was. He could recall how he used to bury his mouth in that spot just at the hollow of her throat where the pulse was warm and exciting beneath his lips, and how it used to drive him wild with longing. Something tightened inside of him, like a noose going around his heart. Damn it, why did he have to remember something like that?

Why did she have to be sitting there looking so painfully vulnerable, so obviously frightened in spite of her stubborn resolve to show him no weakness? Tearing him apart with remembering how it used to be.

So deeply mired was Catherine in her own torturous thoughts that she was unaware at first that the pickup had come to a halt and that Cal had shut off the engine. Gradually, she became aware of the feel of his eyes upon her, guiding her away from her own private agonies and toward him like two beacons in a storm.

In a low voice he uttered, "Are you all right?"

His eyes were no longer smoky dark and brimming with hostility, but were bright and green and beautiful in the moonlight that slashed across his face. In them Catherine saw none of the animosity of before, only a look of deep and familiar concern.

Her guard slipped like a ton of bricks. She drew in a shuddering breath, and in a small voice, whispered, "I was so scared, Cal. So scared."

It was as if he had stepped into a time warp and the last ten years never happened. Here was Cathy looking back at him with tear-shiny eyes, confiding her fears to him the way she used to do . . . His Cathy reaching instinctively out to him in spite of all that reckless pride.

He could remember a time when he'd felt the kind of fear he was seeing now in her dark and lovely eyes. Caused then, as it was now, by a sudden, uncontrollable accident. Almost grudgingly, he said, "I know the feeling. I landed in a hospital bed once. Fortunately, you've escaped with only a cut on your head." His expression softened toward her. "It'll be better in the morning," he told her, even though he knew from experience that that wasn't always the case.

She smiled halfheartedly, unconvinced that she would feel any less desperate in the morning than she felt at this very moment. He'd misunderstood. It wasn't just the accident. That had been merely the catalyst to set off the emotions that were at this very moment colliding within her. Sitting there in that car, with the darkness stalking all around her, she'd felt the one thing it all came down to.

"Alone," she breathed. "I felt so alone."

If it were not for the expression Catherine saw on his face just then, she wouldn't even have been aware that she had spoken out loud.

Alone. The word had such a final, irrevocable sound to it. Cal knew all about being alone. Hell, he'd written the book on it. He stretched his arm out along the back of the seat, fingers stopping within a hair's breadth of her shoulder. His gaze dropped beneath his lashes. "It's not so bad. You get used to it after a while."

Catherine was touched. Perhaps he hadn't misunderstood, after all. Then she remembered something she'd forgotten—like her, Cal had no one. There were no brothers or sisters, both parents and grandparents gone.

"You never married?"

The question had come quite naturally, he could tell that by the utter absence of tension in the soft tones in which it was uttered.

"Me?" He shook his head as he looked away. "No."

She looked at him inquisitively. "There's been no one? In all these years?"

"There was someone a few years back, but it never came close to marriage."

Catherine felt a prick of jealousy to think there had been someone other than herself in his life. "What happened?"

He shrugged, and answered frankly, "The same notion that told me to get involved, also told me I'd better move along."

"You were lucky," said Catherine. "You avoided a loveless marriage. I had to escape from one." She turned away and reached for the doorlatch, but the strong hand that clamped over her shoulder pulled her back to face him.

"Loveless?" he questioned. His eyes were stormy bright, the way they got when she knew he was angry. "Then why'd you do it, Cathy?"

With a protracted groan, she pleaded, "Oh God, Cal, what does it matter?" Who was he to judge her? What made him think that her sins were greater than his own?

His fingers tightened over her flesh. In a tense voice filled with repressed emotion he said, "It doesn't."

She felt herself pulled none too gently into an angry embrace. The tenderness of only minutes ago vanished in a puff of smoke. He kissed her punishingly, as if to confirm just how little anything mattered. Or was it simply to remind her of how little anything had changed? Catherine wasn't sure which. The only things she was certain of at the moment were the press of the hard-muscled chest against her, the scorch of his lips, the thrust of his tongue, all achingly familiar and each action alone capable of rendering her helpless.

Catherine succumbed to the plundering of her mouth, too weak to protest, too tired to care where it would take them. Was this to be it, then? she wondered fleetingly. All that red-hot passion of their youth held in check, only to explode here and now in the front seat of Cal's pickup truck?

Catherine suddenly remembered the night they had come closer than they'd ever come before, burning for each other in the front seat of Angus's VW, which they had borrowed that night to drive into Edmonton to see a movie. She'd been a willing partner that night, an eager participant. There was nothing she would not have given him, that was how much she loved him and burned for him. He'd been the one to insist that they wait. He had teased her about her inability to keep her hands off him, then grew serious and told her that he would indeed be the first to make love to her, but that it would be on their wedding night. It had hurt her, made her even a little angry, particularly when he was the one who usually had to be kept under control.

As fate would have it, he hadn't been the first, and there had been no wedding night, and the memory of something that was never meant to be threw the cold, harsh light of reality over the present situation. Catherine squirmed out of Cal's embrace and skittered across the seat to hug the door with her shoulder.

He had been remembering, too. Things like the front seat of Angus Coleman's '68 Volkswagen bug, the steam of their kisses fogging up the windows, the night she almost gave in, the rock-hard willpower it had taken for him to resist the temptation.

He'd wanted to, god, how he'd wanted to. But she was too special, too precious a prize to risk. No man was going to take advantage of Cathy, not even him. He'd been determined to wait as long as he could. But in the end, he would have her, and he would be the first, and he figured it should be on their wedding night.

For a couple of minutes just now, he'd felt all that again. Felt her acquiescence and his own chemical reaction to it. He also felt the wall of resistance going up again between them. "What is it?" he questioned. "What's the matter?"

"I'm afraid," she said.

"Of me?"

Softly, she admitted, "Of you. Of me. Of this."

She wasn't ready. There were still too many doubts, too much unresolved conflict between them for her to fall into his arms. It was only as she reached for the doorlatch and noticed that the buttons on her blouse were undone, that Catherine realized she'd just had her second close call of the day.

Cal walked her to the porch. "You should see a doctor about that bump on your head," he said.

"It's nothing. I've had worse."

She glanced nervously over her shoulder up at the house. The windows were dark.

"Isn't anyone home?" Cal asked. He, too, sensed the loneliness of the place.

Catherine shook her head. "Ben took Gertie to Red Deer to see her folks. They won't be back until tomorrow afternoon."

He made no move to leave, but kicked absently at the dust with his boot. "Will you be all right tonight?"

"Yes," she answered. Then, "No." And finally, "I don't know."

Great, thought Cal. Here she was, trying to be brave and not succeeding very well. And here he was, trying not to be a sucker for a pair of big brown eyes and not succeeding very well.

"Right. Well, I guess I'd better get going." He turned to leave.

"Cal?"

The sound of her voice softly filling the space between them made him stop.

"I—I know I have no right to ask. But would you . . . could you . . . stay the night?"

He looked at her questioningly, unaware of the glimmer of hope that sprang into his eyes. "But I thought you said—"

"No," she said. "I mean, in Angus's room."

Cal laughed in spite of himself. Wasn't that just like Cathy, vulnerable enough to need him and bold enough to ask? He had to admire her nerve.

But it was more than sheer nerve that had made her ask him to stay the night. He knew from her pale face and wide eyes that she was still shaken up over the accident, and scared. Forget it, Walker, he scoffed to himself. You're dead meat.

"Sure, Cath. I'll stay."

SIX

The hours dragged by, the ticking of eternity, as Catherine tossed and turned in bed unable to find the sleep that would take her away from the horrors of this day. First, the ride into Edmonton, bringing back a host of memories, things she'd almost forgotten of her youth and of her beloved grandfather. Then, the flamboyant Doctor Devlin raising her ire with his supercilious attitude toward her. Next, the accident and the jarring realization of what could happen in less than a heartbeat. And finally, Cal.

His coming along the way he had, the repercussions of the ride home, the thought of him at this very moment asleep just down the hall, and a flock of other, more intimate thoughts about him, all converged upon Catherine to render sleep impossible.

She'd been shocked by the poignant confession of loneliness he'd uttered in the pickup. And it was that, even more than the rake of his lips across hers, that lingered into these late hours to torment her.

It was that very loneliness, sharper and more desperate in the aftermath of her chilling experience on the road, that pervaded Catherine's every thought. Loneliness and need. As she lay atop the mattress with the sheet thrown back from the summer heat, she began to feel the need within her grow to an almost physical ache, until it was indistinguishable from want. In the end, it was not so much a conscious thought as a subliminal longing that guided Catherine through the darkness to his door.

She stood in breathless silence before the door to Angus's bedroom, feeling foolish and anxious and heady and afraid all at the same time. Balling her fist she rapped gently, not too loud in case he was asleep.

She jumped when a soft voice murmured from within, "Come in."

With a trembling hand she turned the doorknob and entered.

The room was wrapped in shadow and half-light. Pearly, vaporized rays of moonlight slanted through the open window to fall in widening planes over the hardwood floor and across the bed.

Cal was sitting up in bed, the pillows propped behind him, one arm crooked lazily behind his head. Starlight played across his bare chest. The only thing that lay between his nakedness and the night was the thin white sheet draped loosely over him, its hem resting comfortably just below his taut stomach, scarcely concealing his modesty. A straight line of black hair ran downward from just below his navel and disappeared beneath the sheet. Catherine's gaze followed its hidden path to the pointed rise in the sheet. She felt the color rush to her face, and was grateful for the darkness that concealed it.

There was a soft huskiness to his voice that spoke to her from out of the mantled night. "I see you couldn't sleep, either."

"No," she murmured. "I couldn't." She realized suddenly how foolish it was for her to be here. Why had she come anyway? Surely, he was asking himself the same question. But short of turning and running from the room, what could she do?

For a split second she thought that if he asked her what she was doing here, she would say she heard a noise outside and was frightened. A little lie couldn't hurt, and would spare her the morbid embarrassment of the truth.

Instead, he ventured, "Why don't you come over here and sit down?"

She hesitated, unable to turn and flee, unable to take that first step forward.

"You don't have to do anything you don't want to do, Cathy."

His deeply-uttered assurance gave her the courage to move noiselessly closer and sit down on the edge of the bed.

Her voice, shy, almost childlike, floated like a feather into the stillness. Eyes downcast, she said, "I didn't thank you before. I want you to know I'm grateful for . . . for everything."

His hand found hers on the sheet and cradled it in the security of his warm, strong fingers. "Catherine, look at me."

Her gaze came up slowly to meet his.

"You don't have to thank me," he said. "At least

not like this. If you're here, it's got to be because you want to be."

He guessed the source of her hesitation, and stressed, "No guarantees. No promises. No excuses. Whatever happens here can disappear with the dawn. It's up to you, Cathy. Whatever you decide."

She succumbed with a smile to the reassurance she had sought from him and received.

Her eyelids fluttered closed as his palms came up to mold themselves to the contours of her face. Delicately, his thumbs traced the line of her brows, her eyelids. Like feathers they brushed her dark lashes and followed the outline of her lips and the sweep of her nose. One hand curled beneath her chin and with gentle pressure urged her head up.

Catherine opened her eyes to an unreadable gaze. There was a stillness about him, a concentration that held him quietly enraptured in the study of her face. His thoughts were unknown to her, yet the weight of them settled heavily upon her. She felt them hovering on the border of her consciousness, absorbing the very essence of her through her flesh, into his mind, his soul. Her lips parted. The movement was so slight as to be barely noticeable, except to one who was watching so intently.

Cal placed the tip of his index finger to Catherine's lips to silence whatever words she'd been about to utter. His raspy, urgent whisper sent waves of anticipation over her.

"Kiss me."

The words, uttered with barely a breath, carried the force of a command that Catherine had no wish to disobey. Turning her face, she placed a kiss upon his warm open palm, another upon his forearm, another still upon his shoulder, his throat, and lastly, his waiting lips.

Cal's arms moved around her like liquid. With gentle strength he pulled her over him and positioned her comfortably beside him on the bed. He hugged her very close and touched his lips to hers lightly, once, twice, feather-soft caresses of sweetness.

The satin nightshirt she was wearing had a sensual slipperiness beneath his palm as it savored the swell of her hip. Beneath the smooth fabric her flesh was warm, soft, giving, pushing upwards against his palm. Her breath quickened when he bent his head and kissed the nipple that peaked beneath the fabric.

"Cathy," he murmured as his tongue made unhurried circles over the satiny fabric. "Say it."

She tangled her hands in his dark hair, moaning as his mouth journeyed back to her face and descended over her lips in a forceful kiss.

In a fluid motion he rolled on top of her. His body was long and hard against the length of hers. He caught her wrists in his hands and pressed them to the mattress. Lifting his head, he gazed with desire-hazed eyes down at her.

"I want to hear you say it."

The throaty whisper thrilled her, yet she held back. A fan of ebony lashes swooped down to mask her eyes. She turned her face to one side, away from his that was only inches away. Her hesitation stretched, becoming painfully obvious.

"Cathy?"

Cal's breath was not against her cheek. She tried to swallow down the lump in her throat but found that she could not. In a ragged voice she said, "Can't this be enough?"

His fingers tightened painfully around her wrists. In a fierce whisper he replied, "No, it's *not* enough."

Catherine closed her eyes in anguish. What did he want her to say? That she loved him? No! Not that! It was lust, nothing more. They'd always been hot for each other.

Her thoughts were swirling madly, like bubbles in a glass of champagne. Cal's breath against her flesh was making her dizzy with desire. He felt warm and solid on top of her. The thrust of his knee between her thighs sent a spasm of pleasure through her, obliterating all thoughts, making the process of thinking meaningless. Desire was rapidly overwhelming her. Her body felt open, empty, begging to be filled.

The urgency within her increased. She reached her hands up to his shoulders and ran her palms along the tight, firm flesh, then across the breadth of his hard chest. His vitality seemed to burn right through his flesh. Everywhere she touched him it heated her hands like an open flame.

A need unlike any Catherine had ever known or thought existed sprang up within her, mingling with earth-shaking desire. This was Cal, whom she'd wanted, desired, craved for ten long years. His big, hard hands were moving down her sides, his thumb toying with her navel as his lips and tongue played with her flesh.

She opened her eyes and looked at him. The scar that slashed across his left cheek gave his handsomeness a lurid appeal. It frightened and compelled her all at once. On impulse she reached up to touch it.

He felt her fingers slide past the rasp of his unshaved chin to the softness of his cheek, where the thin white seam that scarred his face began to throb. He tried to tell himself that just having her like this was enough for him, but he knew it wasn't. He grasped her hand in his and pulled it away from his face.

"Say it."

There was no escaping the obvious, not for either of them. In answer to Cal's almost desperately uttered command, Catherine looked deeply into his eyes and said, "I want you, Cal. God, how I want you."

The words soared through Cal's mind like birds in mad flight. He answered her with a low whimper of desire, whispering against her flesh in unintelligible utterances. A thousand thoughts exploded in his mind. How many nights had he held her like this in his dreams? How pitifully wanting his wildest imaginings had been until now, this moment of revelation, rendering all his dreams lackluster compared to the pandemonium the real thing unleashed in him.

He'd spent ten years waiting for a feeling to come along that would match what he'd felt back then. A feeling such as he had tonight, at this moment, when the myriad loose ends of that feeling all came together in one conscious, physical act. He'd been beginning to think he was the only one who longed for this, until that day on the hillside when he'd tasted in Cathy's kiss a hunger that matched his own. This was what he'd been waiting for all this time, while telling himself that he was better off without it . . . better off without her.

Whatever doubts Cal had as to whether the wait was worth it were put to rest by Catherine's seeking hands and teasing tongue, by the grasping need he felt emanating from her, and by the thought that, even if it was only for this one night, that need was solely for him.

His hand slid beneath her head to grab a handful of dark hair. Lifting her mouth to his, he teased her lips open with little strokes of his tongue. "That'll do for now," he said huskily against her mouth.

He moved rapidly now, sliding the satin nightshirt past her hips and up over her head, exposing her naked flesh to the glow of the moonlight from the window, his hot, wet mouth closing over her breast.

Her own hands, hasty and trembling, pushed the sheet away and began the slow exploration of his body. She'd always thought he had a beautiful body. He was tall, broad-shouldered, small-waisted, with thickly corded thighs, and arms kept strong and well-muscled from ranchwork. She used to like the look of him in a pair of dusty jeans, particularly the way the fabric stretched tightly over his buttocks, and that place just beneath his fly where the denim was worn a little thin from the press of his anatomy.

She'd never seen him naked, though, until right now, when what she saw took her breath away. He was still lean and taut, with not an ounce of fat on him. But he had filled out in his maturity, the extra weight adding muscle and definition and making him look bigger than she remembered him to be.

Cal reveled in her touch upon his rising flesh. He wanted to prolong each caress, to burn upon his senses the ecstasy of being this close to her, this intimate. He wanted to freeze the moment and ride the crest of this wave until eternity settled over him, and it was only with a savage force of will that he was able to hold his exploding passion in check, when it would have been so easy to take quick, deep, driving possession of her and quench the fire that raged inside of him.

With every nerve screaming for release, and the stars peeping in at them through the open window, Cal fulfilled his raging desire, reclaiming every inch of her, memorizing, remembering, discovering new places he had not touched or tasted before, each thrust bringing him closer and closer to what he'd given up for lost.

She clasped him about the waist and her hips rose to meet his, higher and higher until at last she felt him arch for a final blinding thrust, and felt her own body shudder in answer.

It was a while before Catherine came to herself and remembered where she was and who was laying naked next to her.

Her head was nestled in the crook of his arm. "Cal," she murmured, touching his sweaty hair, "what are you thinking?"

He drew in a deep breath and let it out slowly. How could he tell her what he was thinking without sounding like a complete idiot? "To tell you the truth, I was trying not to think."

She sighed and burrowed closer against him. Yes, it was best not to think.

He felt the stirrings of renewed desire and drew her closer to him, but she was already asleep, her bare bottom pressed up against his half-swollen maleness. He made no move to touch her. Instead, he just cradled her in his arms, until he sensed that she was far, far out of reach, and then he gently pulled his arm from beneath her and got out of bed.

For several minutes he stood by the side of the

bed looking down at the soundly-sleeping woman. Her face was breathtakingly lovely in repose. As he studied the smooth line of her brow, the shadow of her long lashes against her cheek, her lips that were red and softly swollen from his rough kisses, he felt a softening of the bitterness that had been eating away at him all these years, a wavering in his determination to hate her. It was only the imperceptible throbbing of his cheek as it grew to a conscious ache that made Cal remember just what the woman he'd just made love to was capable of. She had used him tonight, hadn't she? And he had let her, proving to his shame and regret what a fool he really was.

Well, she was safe now, he reasoned. There was no need for him to stay. She would never even know he was gone. And besides, she would probably be grateful for it in the morning.

He dressed quickly and closed the door quietly behind him.

The next morning Catherine was in the kitchen making breakfast, jabbing at a strip of frying bacon with a fork while severely reproaching herself for the moment of inexcusable weakness that had driven her into Cal's arms last night.

It had been late, she'd been traumatized in the wake of the accident, and didn't know any better, she rationalized. Out of her mind was more like it, for the way she had opened herself up to him.

He'd taken advantage of her, that's what he'd done. He should have known that she was not herself last night. How could he have used her moments of weakness against her the way he had? And to leave the way he did, like a thief in the night, without even so much as a good-bye. But that was like him, wasn't it, to leave without saying good-bye?

While the bacon was frying in the pan, Catherine beat angrily at the eggs in the bowl. Her mind, however, was nowhere on scrambled eggs and bacon. It was trapped in thoughts of last night and of what it had felt like to be in Cal's arms.

He had said to her that whatever happened between them could disappear with the dawn if she wanted it to. Well, here it was, well past dawn, in fact. And her skin was still flushed all over, her lips felt bruised, and there was a mild abrasion on her neck from where his stubble-spiked chin had rubbed against the tender flesh. She'd been crazy to believe him. But then, in the state she'd been in last night, she would have believed anything, even that he still maybe cared for her. She thought she'd felt it in his touch, heard it in the rasp of his voice against her flesh, sensed it in the desperate, almost brutal way he had clung to her, but she realized now that she must have imagined it. If he truly cared for her, he wouldn't have left, and she would be cooking breakfast this morning for two instead of one.

It was all for the best, she supposed. The last thing she needed was to get involved all over again with Cal Walker. With all of her other problems, this was one big one she didn't need.

"Smells like something's burning."

Catherine whirled around to the deep timbre of Cal's voice from behind. He was standing in the doorway as calm as you please, jeans slung a little low on his hips, the sleeves of his shirt spanning the muscles of his upper arms that were folded across at his chest. What was he doing here? Catherine groaned inside. Had he come to gloat? The scowl on his face did not bode well.

The sight of her froze the expression on Cal's face. She was wearing a robe of silk crepe de chine in a delicate floral pattern of lilacs and roses on an ivory background. It was the last thing he'd ever thought to see on a sheep ranch. No doubt purchased from an expensive Boston department store, it was classy and unexpected, and so like her.

She had that wild, disheveled look of a woman who'd only recently arisen from a warm bed. His gaze dipped to the folds of her robe that had come open across her bare leg, exposing a smooth-skinned calf.

Cal was astonished by his body's lightning-quick response, and hoped it didn't show. He nodded impatiently past her and said, "The bacon, Cathy, you're burning the bacon."

Crisp, black strips that bore no resemblance to anything edible lay sizzling in the frying pan. Catherine grasped a fork on the counter and attempted to spear them. The fat sputtered and hissed. A burst of hot fat splattered on the back of her hand, and she dropped the fork with a little yelp of pain.

With a rapid stride he was beside her. In one smooth motion he doused the flame, moved the pan off the heat, and reached past her to turn on the faucet. Then he took Catherine's hand unexpectedly in his and held it under the cold running water.

"Where's that stuff you always use?"

Catherine was so stunned by the unnerving sensation caused by the ice-cold water and Cal's hot grip that she failed to notice the familiarity implied in his choice of words. Looking up at him with large, questioning eyes she asked, "Stuff?"

"You know. That stuff in the bottle."

She knew he was referring to the aloe vera gel her grandmother used to keep in the kitchen for burns. "It's in the refrigerator."

She had taken her grandmother's remedy for burns one step further by placing it in cold storage, and was glad for it when Cal spilled some into his palm and then applied it to the back of her hand.

The cold gel worked speedily to relieve the sting. Now, if there was only some way to ease the fires that burned from within.

"Thank you. That's m–much better," she stumbled, withdrawing her hand from his. She busied herself with sponging up the grease that had splattered all over the stove, saying without looking at him, "I didn't expect to see you today."

"Didn't expect to see me, or didn't want to?"

There was only the slightest hesitation in her movement as she continued to scrub the stove. "Both," she said. She didn't have to be looking at him to know that his luminous green eyes had darkened.

Cal snorted derisively and said, "To the point, aren't you?"

Catherine tossed the sponge into the sink and turned to look at him as she wiped her hands on a dish towel. That ominous look he was wearing had never scared her before, and it didn't frighten her now. All it did was annoy her.

She sighed impatiently and said, "Long and flowery, brief and to the point, what difference does it make? How ever you say it, the truth hurts."

Something in her tone should have warned him, but he damned the consequences and plunged right in. "Truth? That's funny coming from you, Cathy, you know that?"

Her chin tilted up at him in that infuriatingly defiant way of hers. "I've never been afraid of the truth," she asserted. "No matter how much it hurts, I can tell you that lies hurt much more. At least the truth leaves you with some dignity. Lies leave you with nothing."

He smiled caustically into those dark eyes that were burning up at him from out of a flushed face. "Is that so? All right, I guess we're sticking strictly to the truth this morning. I presume I get my turn at it, too? Okay, so far, we've established that you don't want to see me. Is that just for today, or forever? I'd like some clarification on that point, if you don't mind. And remember, we're speaking the truth here."

Catherine stiffened at the ridicule in his tone. It would have been easy to toss off a caustic remark, to tell him how reprehensible he was and that she didn't want to see him *ever*. To stoop to a lie if she must, if only to wipe that smirk off his face. But however much it may have appealed to her to be cruel at this moment, it was in her nature to rely on her cleverness instead.

"You want the truth?" she stormed up at him. "All right. I didn't want to see you . . . today."

The brightness flared in his eyes. "Does that mean that you wanted to see me *after* today?"

"It doesn't matter what I mean," she said sourly. "You wanted the truth, so there it is. And you, Cal? Didn't you say you wanted equal time?"

He sensed the trap when it was too late. "Yeah. Sure," he answered.

"Okay. Then tell me why, when I woke up this morning, you were nowhere to be found."

He hadn't expected the clever table-turning. When he had demanded no less than the truth from her, how could he offer anything less than the truth himself?

Cal didn't want to admit that he had allowed himself to be seduced last night by Catherine's vulnerability, so he said, "I didn't think it would make any difference to you." It was the truth, but only a small part of it.

Those big brown eyes looked at him petulantly. "You could have said something. You know, goodnight, see you around, have a nice life. Surely, you say *some*thing to the women you seduce before you walk out the door."

"I don't seduce women," he exclaimed. "And I didn't seduce you. If I remember correctly, it was you who knocked on my door in the middle of the night, not the other way around."

Catherine cringed. Did he have to remind her of that? "And you were the one who said that it could all disappear with the dawn. 'Whatever you decide', isn't that what you said, Cal?"

"Sure, I said it. So what?"

"So what are you doing here this morning?"

His eyes fixed tightly on hers. What could he say? That last night she had made him feel something he thought no longer existed? That he'd come racing over here this morning like a stag in rut just to make love to her again whether she liked it or not? That he was falling in love with her all over again in spite of every inner warning not to? That was a laugh, he thought bitterly, falling in love with her all over again. If last night proved anything at all, it was that he had never really stopped.

Cal galvanized his defenses against her. It was hormonal, he reminded himself, and lust had nothing to do with love.

"I came to tell you that you had no brake fluid."

Catherine blinked at him. "What?"

"Your car. I drove out to look at it earlier. There wasn't any brake fluid. That's why the brakes failed."

"Brake fluid? I don't understand."

"Someone let it get down too low. Do you understand me now?"

Any sarcasm was lost on Catherine as her mind began to spin. No brake fluid? Was that true? Had Ben let it get down too low? She didn't want to believe that Ben had been responsible for the accident, yet as much as she may have hated admitting it to Cal, her misgivings over her foreman, which had been mounting steadily over the past weeks, were turning now toward suspicion. Catherine didn't know what to think.

"I'm telling you, Cathy, you'd better have a talk with that foreman of yours."

The accusing tone of Cal's voice lit the spark on Catherine's temper. "First of all, you're presuming that it was Ben's fault, when you don't know that at all. And in the second place, I don't come over to Pitchfork and tell you how to run things, Cal, so I'd appreciate it if you wouldn't do that with me. *I'll* handle my problems, thank you."

"So, you admit there's a problem?"

Catherine turned away in a rustle of silk. "The only problem I have at the moment, Cal, is you."

She was as hardheaded as that old Scotsman had been. Didn't she realize that she could have been hurt badly, or worse, going off the side of the road like she did? She had a problem, all right, only she was too damned stubborn to admit it.

He threw up his hands in disgust and said, "All right. Fine. Do what you want. Just don't let me run into McFarland."

"In that case, perhaps you should leave," she said as she scraped the remains of her uneaten breakfast into the trash. "He and Gertie are due back any time now."

But when she turned back, he was still standing there. "Was there something else you wanted to say, Cal?"

He wasn't sure if that was a question or a challenge. "No," he muttered. "Nothing."

"If you'll excuse me, then, I have to take a shower and go to work. I've wasted too much time already."

Was that all he was to her, a waste of time? And last night? Was that a waste of time, too? In that brief time spent with her in his arms, he had sensed her need, not just for the clasp of a warm body but for *his* warm body. Had he only imagined her surrender? The iciness he was met with this morning seemed to suggest wishful thinking on his part. He turned to leave.

"What? No good-bye, Cal?"

The sound of her voice stopped him when he reached the doorway. There was the distinct threat of something dangerous in the sweet, husky tones.

"Ah, well, some things never change, I suppose," Cathy said.

He turned back to her in a rapid motion. "If you're referring to last night, all right damn it, I was wrong for leaving the way I did. For that I apologize. I just didn't think—"

"I'm referring to ten years ago."

He glared at her, enraged that she would dare to bring up the past. And she didn't even have the facts straight! "What are you talking about?" he exclaimed.

"I'm talking about ten years ago when you didn't even say good-bye."

"*I* didn't say good-bye? What has ten years in Boston done to you, fried your brains? You were always a smart girl, Cathy. Don't tell me you've turned dumb. Somehow I don't buy it."

"Are you saying that a smart woman doesn't deserve the courtesy of a good-bye?" she cried with indignation.

"Of course not. What I'm saying is, I didn't say good-bye because *I* didn't leave. *You* did."

Catherine's fury was lost in a half-smothered gasp. She opened her mouth to speak, but she was so furious that the words wouldn't come. "I . . . I . . ." She gulped in a breath of air and blurted out, "*I* left? Oh, that's just great, Cal. And did I take twenty-five thousand dollars with me?"

"Twenty-five thousand dollars is a far sight less than what you married," scoffed Cal. "I hear the guy's worth millions."

"His money, not mine. Look around you, Cal. Do I look like *I'm* worth millions?"

"Oh, that's right," he said, as if suddenly remembering, "You didn't take any money from him when you left."

"Accept," Catherine heatedly corrected. "I didn't *accept* any money from him. I don't *take* things, Cal."

You took my heart, he wanted to say, but didn't. He shook his head with a dismal gesture that made Catherine bristle, and said, "You can bet Angus had something to say about your marrying that . . . that Yankee."

That Yankee. Angus's very words. She could even hear the burr of his Scottish accent.

"Don't try to change the subject," said Catherine. "At least I didn't take a bribe to do what I did."

"I never took a bribe in my life. You don't know what you're talking about."

He had that obstinate, defensive look that might have made her almost believe him. If only the facts didn't prove otherwise. If only there was some way to go back in time and erase the mistakes. If only her heart would stop aching over his betrayal.

Catherine pulled in a supportive breath and looked bravely into those eyes that hedged somewhere between light and dark. "It's no use, Cal. I know about the money. My father told me."

It had never been any secret that Ellis Randolph hated Cal, considering the son of a cattle rancher an unworthy suitor for his daughter. They used to laugh over it, though, vowing that nothing, not even Cathy's powerful father, would keep them apart. Cal wasn't surprised when Ellis showed up at Pitchfork and offered him twenty-five thousand dollars to get out of Cathy's life. He'd told Randolph to take a hike, albeit in slightly more salty language. He made an enemy of his future father-in-law that day, but little did Cal suspect where it would all lead.

Cal had thought the matter settled, but he had underestimated the formidable Ellis Randolph. Days later, Ellis Randolph reappeared at Pitchfork, the big gray limousine looking strangely absurd parked in the gravel driveway. He had come to inform Cal of Cathy's marriage to a Boston businessman. The news had hit Cal with the impact of a fist in the solar plexus.

Bitterly, Cal responded, "That sounds like him."

"He was only trying to protect me."

"Against what?" he scoffed. "Himself?"

"No. Against a man who would take twenty-five thousand dollars to get out of my life."

"Take— *What?*" He was at her side in a blindingly fast movement that took her by surprise. "I never took that money," he asserted. He glared down into her brown eyes, daring her to refute it.

Catherine backed away from him. "But he told me . . ." Something shuddered inside of her. She tore her eyes from his and looked about, as if the understanding to all of this lay somewhere in the room. In a trembling, confused voice she said, "He told me you took the money."

Flatly, he replied, "Yeah, well, he lied."

She knew her father hadn't wanted her to marry Cal. He'd made no secret of it during their many arguments. She knew also that he was ruthless in his business dealings, but she had never imagined that his ruthlessness would extend to her. Was it possible, she wondered aghast, that he had lied to her about Cal taking that money?

She looked so damned pitiful standing there with

her brown eyes clouded with confusion and a look of pained shock on her face that he could almost feel sorry for her. Grudgingly, he asked, "Why do you look so hurt? I'm the one who should be hurt. It's not every day you learn that the girl you're supposed to marry has run off to marry someone else. It's like you said, the truth hurts."

He saw her face go pale in the sunlight that streamed in through the kitchen window. She was shaking her head slowly from side to side as if she was hearing this for the first time and couldn't believe it.

"I didn't—" she began. Then, "Oh my God." The words, a groan of agony as Catherine's incomprehension turned to cold, hard understanding. There was an expression of utter disbelief on her face. "How could you think I would do such a thing?" Her eyes burned strongly into his. "I loved you. God, I loved you. How could I even think of another man when there was you?"

"You married someone else, though, didn't you?" Cal shot back.

"Yes!" Catherine cried. "Yes, I married someone else." Hot tears welled in her eyes. "Don't you understand? He told me you took the money. There was nothing left for me after that. I waited and waited and you didn't come back. I would have had you back even if you *had* taken the money. If you didn't know that, Cal Walker, then you didn't know me."

"You sure didn't wait very long," he charged.

Her dark and angry gaze clashed with his. "I acted rashly. I made a mistake and I paid for it. But what difference does that make? You were gone, weren't you?"

"Yes, damn it! Because he told me you'd run off to marry someone else."

Catherine felt sick. A knot the size of a walnut lodged in her throat, making it difficult for her to breathe. "And you believed that?"

"He said you'd already left for your honeymoon," said Cal defensively, but he could feel his defenses crumbling all around him even as he spoke.

If there was ever any doubt in either of their minds as to whether Catherine's father had lied to each of them, it was put to rest with this terrible discovery that they had *both* been lied to.

Ellis Randolph had apparently used their love against them for his own manipulative ends. Determined to drive them apart at any cost, his plan had worked. Catherine left Alberta, convinced that Cal had taken the money. And Cal, having been told that she'd run off to marry another man, turned his back on the twenty-five thousand dollars and Pitchfork, and disappeared.

Cal felt as if he'd been hit by a Mack truck. He grasped the kitchen counter for support, knuckles whitening under the strength it took to stay on his feet.

Catherine could not speak for the lump in her throat and the tears that spilled silently down her cheeks.

All they could do was stand there as the truth descended over them, stunning each of them with its grim reality. Ten years of wondering, of what ifs, of pain and anger and bitterness all summed up in this one moment of crushing truth as Catherine and Cal learned that neither had ever been untrue to the other.

SEVEN

"Yes, I understand. Well, thank you Doctor Devlin, I'll wait for your call. What's that? Oh, of course, I mean, Drew. As I was saying, I'll wait for your call."

Catherine dropped the receiver back into the cradle and glared down at the phone on her night table as if it were the enemy. "Patient," she huffed. "He wants me to be patient." She expelled a breath of frustration. She couldn't afford to be patient, not when a count of the flock showed the loss of three more sheep since she'd driven to Edmonton. That was what, seven, eight days ago? She ran her fingers through her hair, sweeping the chestnut locks from her eyes, and shook her head dismally, thinking that she didn't even know what day this was.

Downstairs in the kitchen Gertie was making preparations for dinner when she heard the tap of Catherine's footsteps on the stairs.

Catherine tried to summon a lightheartedness she

did not truly feel when she entered the kitchen and saw Gertie at the counter. "What's for dinner?"

Gertie did not fail to see the troubled expression shadowing Catherine's pretty features. "Veal stew steeped in gravy with potatoes and vegetables," she answered. She knew it was one of Catherine's favorites. Maybe that and the apple pie she was making for dessert would help put back the pounds Catherine had lost in the last few weeks. With those long legs and slender frame it gave her a coltish look that no doubt had its appeal to men—she'd seen the way that Cal Walker had looked at her—but as far as Gertie was concerned, Catherine had grown downright skinny and needed some fattening up. Now, if only there was something that would put the smile back in her eyes, the woman thought as she peeled the Granny Smiths.

Gertie liked Catherine, perhaps because she saw through Catherine's serious veneer to the warmth and courage underneath. If only Catherine and Ben would stop arguing, he would see it, too. But Gertie's husband was a stubborn man, and far too proud in the bargain; not the kind of man who admitted to being wrong. In the Coleman woman, he'd met someone just as proud and pigheaded as he was. Things between them hadn't exactly gone well from the start. But lately, they'd really been locking horns. If the last several nights were any indication, dinner tonight promised to be a tense affair.

Catherine likewise had grown fond of her housekeeper, and often wondered how it was possible for a woman as warm and likable as Gertie to be married to a man as reticent and belligerent as Ben. Just the thought of Ben sent a shudder of apprehension through Catherine. She'd heard him earlier driving in the sheep when she'd been on the phone with Devlin. A glance out the window to the dust clouds that had not yet settled confirmed that he was back.

Gertie heard the familiar creaking of the hinges and the bang of the screen door as Catherine went out, and she knew that it would be only a matter of minutes before angry voices would rise from beyond the window.

These days most herders used motorcycles. Ben even knew one foreman who rounded up his flocks on a shiny Suzuki dirt bike. The best Ben could hope for, though, was Bing, the Coleman steed, who sometimes did what Ben asked him to and sometimes didn't. The animal was as stubborn as his owner was, Ben griped to himself. Thank goodness for Sam, the sheepdog, who, on command, would run around the sheep, taking great delight in his ability to bully them. Agile and wiry, Sam easily did the work of two farmhands. Were it not for the Coleman sheepdog, Ben would never have gotten the sheep in today.

At the sound of Sam's bark, Ben looked up to see Catherine approaching. The dog's tail set to wagging as he ran to greet her.

Catherine gave Sam an affectionate pat on the head. At the fence, she unlatched the gate and stepped into the pen. Her gaze moved slowly, thoughtfully over the flock as she waded in among them. Being surrounded by all these gentle creatures was always a strange experience. They were surprisingly quiet, and together they made a hushed rustle as they moved from one pen to another. She frowned. Their numbers were dwindling and she didn't know how to stop it.

She paused midway across the pen to look at Ben who was now hunched over the engine of the derelict pickup truck with a wrench in his hand.

"I just spoke to Devlin," she announced. "There's no word yet."

He glanced over at her. Standing in the middle of the pen she looked lost surrounded by the sea of white, and for a moment he felt almost sorry for her. "Autopsies don't take this long," he said.

Catherine rolled her eyes and replied, a bit testily, "Well, this one does."

He had made no attempt to hide his objection to her preferring Drew Devlin over the veterinarian he had chosen in Leduc. That was fair enough, thought Catherine. The man was entitled to his opinion. But his constant questioning of her judgment was beginning to grate on her nerves. Why did he insist on treating her as if she were a stranger, when she'd been raised in these parts and knew them certainly as well as, and probably better than, he did? Nor was she a stranger to the hard work that sheep ranching demanded. She was Angus Coleman's granddaughter, after all.

She waded through the sea of white back toward the gate, secured it behind her, and walked to where Ben was working.

"Is something wrong with the truck?" she inquired.

"Nothing I can't handle," he replied.

The truck looked like a rolling urban renewal project sorely in need of bodywork and a paint job, but at least it ran. They had gone back for the station wagon the day after the accident, when Ben and Gertie got back from Red Deer, and towed it home behind the truck. There'd been no time at all to even look at the car this week. Catherine glanced at it now as it sat under the shade of the trees, a constant reminder of a terrifying experience.

She looked back at Ben and asked with all due innocence, "You don't think the brake fluid might be down too low, do you?"

He shot her an unappreciating look over his shoulder. "Did Devlin say when there *would* be word?" he asked.

Catherine wasn't surprised by his abrupt shifting of the subject. Every attempt she had made thus far to bring up the subject of the brake fluid had been met defensively by Ben.

"He said something about the lab over at the university." She shrugged, for the truth was she herself didn't understand why it was taking this long. "Who knows?"

"We could've used that vet over in Leduc," said Ben. "The one I was using before."

"Before what, Ben? Before I came?" Her voice rose in spite of her effort to control it. "That is what you mean, isn't it?"

Ben met her angry gaze with his own heated one. "I mean, the one we were using before we started using Devlin."

"What have you got against him?" Catherine demanded.

"What have *you* got against the vet in Leduc?" he shot back.

Catherine threw up her hands to head off the inevitable argument that had become unbearably familiar. "Look, all I know is something's getting past Sam.

And it's not wolves, and it's not coyotes. Sam wouldn't let them anywhere near his flocks, you know that as well as I do.''

Sam, whose expression had turned tentative at the flaring of the human voices, gave an uncertain wag of the tail at the mention of his name and slinked away unnoticed.

''It's got to be something we can't see,'' Catherine argued. ''Like viral bacteria. If it *is* viral bacteria, we've got a problem. Devlin's supposed to be the best there is. I don't have the time to waste on anything less.''

Her use of the word I as opposed to we told him plainly who was boss. ''And how do you expect to pay him?'' Ben challenged. ''Devlin doesn't come cheap.''

Catherine had had it. Whipping her kid gloves from the back pocket of her jeans, she jammed her hands into them, snapping back, ''That's *my* problem, Ben, not yours,'' and strode angrily past him toward the barn.

Moments later, Bing came tearing from the barn with Catherine astride his bare back, her legs wrapped around the horse's muscular girth, gloved hands clutching fistsful of coarse mane. The dust flew up from those flying hooves as they galloped right past Ben, who watched wide-mouthed and resentful at Bing responding to Catherine the way he'd never done for him.

Catherine rode as hard and fast as she could, not caring where she was going. The ranch disappeared behind her, and she spurred her horse harder and faster, her head down to the horse's neck, the mane whipping at her eyes. She was miles from home when she finally straightened up and slowed the pace. She wasn't concerned about getting lost. If given his head, she knew that Bing would find his way back.

She rode deep into the foothills where there were no arrogant men to rile her, no resentful eyes to watch her, no need to prove anything to anyone. She needed to be alone to think, to sort things out, to find somewhere in the majesty around her relief from the doubts that plagued her.

In the days following Catherine's fateful drive into Edmonton, she'd arisen early every morning and worked tirelessly long past dusk. Late at night Gertie would find her holed up in the den, her dark hair falling all about her face as she bent over the ledgers, juggling figures, cutting corners, devising ways to stretch every penny to its fullest. Long past midnight she would trudge exhausted up to bed.

Gertie scolded her on the way she was pushing herself, but only Catherine knew that the real reason she was throwing herself into her work with such a frenzy was to avoid thinking about Cal.

She foolishly hoped that if she made herself tired enough, the safety of sleep would shield her from the thoughts that tormented her during the daylight hours. Yet, no matter how deeply Catherine slept, she could not elude it. Whichever way she turned, even in slumber, the truth was there to haunt her. Not just the truth about Cal's innocence, but the truth about her own weakness, and his, which had led them both to believe the wicked lies. It brought with it a deep sense of shame for having believed Cal guilty of such a betrayal. And even now, knowing the truth, not fully believing him.

The fact of the matter was that Catherine had grown used to distrusting Cal Walker, even hating him at times. It was a ten-year-old habit that she was finding painfully hard to break. So hard, in fact, that she had even refused Cal's call, pretending not to be home by giving frantic hand signals to Gertie who answered the phone. It was a stupid thing to do, especially considering that in her heart she longed to hear his voice. Several times she had even picked up the phone in her bedroom and started to dial his number, only to hang up like a frightened schoolgirl, not knowing what she would say to him.

She would never forget that look on his face the afternoon the truth had been revealed. That searching expression in his green eyes as if he half expected her to pretend that the last ten years had never happened. How could she make him understand that it wasn't possible to just pick up where they left off ten years ago, as if nothing had happened? Something *did* happen, and neither the startling discovery of the truth, nor one night of need spent in his arms could erase ten years of longing.

Catherine slid from Bing's back and allowed him to graze while she sat for a long time immersed in thought with her back pressed against the trunk of a white-bark pine. Just as she had learned during those ten years that all the longing in the world wouldn't bring Cal back, she was finding out now that it wouldn't save the ranch. At this point, things were looking grim.

She used to ride into the foothills like this whenever something was bothering her. In the shadow of the towering Rockies, dwarfed by the splendor around her, even the biggest problems somehow seemed small. She sat now beneath the tree watching the growing twilight fire the sky with purple, and sure enough, she could feel the tension slowly ebbing from her body. A calmness pervaded the still summer air. How could things be that bad when she was surrounded by all this beauty?

The mountains rose in sawtoothed patterns almost seven thousand feet high to disappear into the clouds. High above the treeline, among the gusting winds, the land resembled the Arctic tundra where lichen and scrub grasses struggled for a toehold during the short growing season. Midway down the mountain-sides the winds were calmer and the more moderate temperature supported thick stands of alpine fir, spruce, and pine. On the slopes and in valley bottoms, such as the one Catherine sat daydreaming in now, there were cottonwoods and birch trees, red squirrels and chipmunks, elk and deer, goats and, yes, sheep. Overhead, the perennially blue Albertan sky had grown smoky with the approach of dusk, and with dusk came a hardening of her will.

This rough and untamed land was as much in her blood as it had been in her grandfather's. She splayed her hand atop the earth and gathered up the soil. This was Angus's fertile soil filling her palm with its cool, dark promise. Her soil, her promise. From the pine-studded peaks that surrounded her, Catherine drew her courage and vowed not to give it up without a fight.

Paradoxically, while she was more than ever determined in her struggle to save the ranch, she was incapable of coming to terms over Cal. The green-eyed cattleman had Catherine feeling as if she was on a roller coaster. One part of her never wanted to see him again. Another, deeper part of her knew she would die if she did not.

Catherine returned home when dusk had settled and dinner was cold. Gertie greeted her at the door with a worried expression.

"I know," Catherine said guiltily, "I missed dinner. I'm sorry, Gertie."

The woman smiled to see that aside from looking tired, Catherine seemed none the worse for wear for the way she'd torn out of there earlier. "I can heat something up for you," she offered.

"I'm beat. I think I'll just go on upstairs."

"How about a piece of apple pie?"

Catherine wavered. She'd always been a sucker for homemade apple pie. "Do we have any vanilla ice cream to go with it?"

Gertie's face brightened. "I'll be right back." She was halfway to the kitchen when she suddenly remembered something and turned back to Catherine with a slightly apprehensive look. "Ben said he wanted to see you when you got back. He's in the den."

The thought of pie *a la mode* flew right out of Catherine's mind. Ah yes, Ben. She supposed she owed him an apology.

"You wanted to see me?" There was no animosity in her tone, only an unmistakable weariness that drew his head up from the newspaper he was reading.

He put the paper aside and looked at her from the easy chair. "Devlin called. The results are in."

The weariness fled as she came forward quickly. "And?"

"You were right," he said grudgingly. "The sheep you took in to him died of a virus."

Catherine felt no triumph in having guessed correctly, only an immense sense of relief in knowing at last what was killing her sheep. But relief turned swiftly to concern.

"What kind of virus?" she questioned.

"Sheep tick."

Her brows drew together questioningly. She wasn't aware of any unusual outbreaks of sheep ticks this season. She might lose one or two animals to the pests, but more than half a dozen? Something about this whole thing bothered her, but she couldn't put her finger on it.

"Did you ever mention anything to Devlin about the sheep we've lost?" she asked him.

"No," he replied. "But I'm not surprised if he knows. News travels fast in these parts."

That had to be it, she concluded. How else would the veterinarian have known about the sheep they'd lost when she hadn't told him? Of course, that didn't explain what made Ben so sure that Devlin knew when she hadn't told him anything either.

Upstairs in the privacy of her room, Catherine told herself that she just wanted to hear it for herself, that it had nothing to do with not believing Ben, when she dialed information and asked the operator for Drew Devlin's home number. Her call was answered by the housekeeper who informed her that Doctor Devlin had gone out of town for several days.

"But he couldn't have called more than a couple of hours ago," Catherine told the woman. "I must speak with him. Can you tell me where he's gone? Oh, I see. Will you tell him then that Catherine Coleman called and that I'd like to speak to him as soon as he gets in? Thank you."

She hung up, her frustration growing by leaps and bounds. If her sheep were dying from a virus caused by the sheep tick, there was no time to lose. And it did not do her patience any good to learn that her vet had gone fishing.

The next day when Ben brought in another dead ewe, Catherine just stared down at the animal, feeling helpless and enraged. To Ben she said, "Get out the shears."

The cool darkness inside the shearing shed was broken by shafts of soft gray light when they carried the animal inside. Clumps of wool lay forgotten on the wide-planked floor. Overhead, cobwebs hung lifelessly off the beams. Things were always crazy here at shearing time. Catherine had always loved watching the brawny shearers haul the frightened sheep onto the floor, and at breakneck speed clip them clean, then thrust them out into the daylight looking half their original size. This shearing season she'd be lucky if she could afford to hire any shearers at all, but Catherine wasn't thinking about that right now as she knelt over the dead animal with the shears in her hand.

From overhead Ben complained, "That won't prove anything."

"If there's a tick on this sheep, I'm going to find it."

"And if you don't find one?"

"Then it'll have left its mark."

Sarcastically, he observed, "You sound like you don't believe the autopsy report."

"I don't know what to believe any more," said

Catherine. She looked up at him then and added pointedly, "Or who."

Her gaze dropped back to the dead animal on the floor. "But you're right, this won't prove anything." She rose to her feet and dusted off the knees of her jeans. "Give me a hand, would you? I want to get her into the truck."

Ben inquired stiffly, "Taking her to Devlin?"

"No, Devlin's out of town. I'm taking her somewhere else."

His expression changed. Was she finally seeing it his way? "I doubt the truck'll make it all the way to Leduc," he pointed out.

But whatever small triumph Ben was feeling was squashed in the next moment when Catherine replied, "I'm not taking her to Leduc. I'm taking her to Pitchfork."

EIGHT

Cal was feeling light in his head and dead on his feet as he struggled under the blazing sun to repair a section of fence in the east corral. He worked bare chested, having pulled off his shirt earlier and tossed it irritably aside when it was soaked clear through with perspiration. Even the bandanna he wore tied around his neck had absorbed all the moisture it would hold, allowing rivulets of sweat to snake unchecked down his broad back. Glistening drops of perspiration fell from the tips of his dark hair to dot the ground. His face was streaked with sweat and grime, and fixed in a look of hard determination.

Catherine approached unnoticed, unable to take her eyes from him. Struggling to sink a fence post into the ground, muscles straining against the hot sun, he looked the epitome of man against the land.

In spite of his unsmiling expression, there was a familiar quality about him that drew her quietly closer to observe him. Her gaze lingered on his striking profile that she knew so well, on the strong line of his jaw, the straight nose, the sweep of dark lashes that concealed eyes which she knew would be bright green in the sunlight. Even the scar that slashed arrogantly across his cheek seemed curiously familiar to her.

Her attention moved slowly downward to the corded neck and the leanly-muscled shoulders that flexed and strained with every movement. And lower still, to the sun-browned flesh of his chest that was streaked with sweat and glistening in the sunshine. There had always been an inexorable magnetism to his appeal. He was all heat and energy, like fire, she thought, warming her inside, burning her up if she got too close. Struck by his hair-trigger sexuality, she struggled to maintain her composure as she came slowly forward.

"Care for a drink?"

Cal glanced up sharply at the sound of her voice. His movements ground to a halt upon seeing her. His eyes took in everything about her at once. She moved with that long and easy stride that had always turned him on. As she came closer, he could see strands of chestnut hair curled in damp ringlets against the sides of her face, which was flushed from the heat. The quarter-mile walk from the house under this hot sun sent beads of moisture trickling down the front of her T-shirt, matting the damp fabric to her flesh. Cal groaned inwardly. Why did he have to notice something like that?

"Millie told me I'd find you here. She asked me to bring you this." She stepped closer and offered him a canteen.

Cal propped the shovel he'd been using against the

fence post, pulled off his work gloves, and reached across the broken fence. His strong hands, browned by the sun, moved gracefully in spite of the callouses on his palms as he unscrewed the cap. He tilted his head back and took several long swallows of water, then leaned forward and poured some over his head before replacing the cap and handing the canteen back to Catherine. When he did, his hand brushed hers. It was barely a touch, lasting no more than a second, yet Catherine felt as if she'd been struck by a live wire.

"What brings you here?" he asked.

"I've lost more sheep."

"I see." He reached for the shovel, put his foot up on it and plunged it into the earth. "For a minute there, Cathy," he said as he worked, "I thought maybe you'd come by for another reason. Sheep, is it? Okay, if you say so. And what does that have to do with me?"

She hadn't expected this to be easy and knew that evasion would only make it worse. Candidly, she replied, "I need your help."

He dropped the shovel to the ground and picked up the heavy wooden post. The muscles bulged in his biceps as he positioned it in place. "How so?"

"I've brought one of the dead animals. I'd like you to have your vet take a look at it."

Cal stepped back to survey his handiwork, running a bare forearm across his forehead as he did. Slightly out of breath he asked, "What's the matter with your own vet?"

"He's out of town and won't be back for several days. I can't wait that long."

Something in her tone made him eye her closely. "What is it?"

She gave an uncertain shrug. "It could be a virus. Sheep tick, maybe."

Cal let out a low whistle. "Man, Cathy, sheep tick. That could be bad. Angus lost nearly half his flock from that outbreak years ago. Remember?"

"Only too well," she replied. "I've lost one to it that I know of. It could be an isolated incident, or it could mean . . ." She could not voice the dreaded possibility.

"C'mon," he said, "let's go get it and bring it around to the barn."

Back at the house Cal went on ahead to the barn, as Catherine drove the pickup around back and then waited while he lifted the bundle out and carried it inside. He reappeared a few minutes later and joined her beside the truck.

"It'll be a couple of days," he said. "We're in the middle of breeding season, and I've got this bull on loan from the Lacombe place, and . . ."

"Cal?"

He stopped his rambling. "Yes?"

"I just wanted to say thank you."

He knew it must have taken a lot for her to come here today. The plain and simple expression of gratitude touched him. He placed his foot up on the chrome bumper of the pickup and said, "I called you a few nights ago."

Her dark lashes swept down to hide a guilty look. "I know. I was home."

He smiled mischievously and said, "I know."

Catherine tossed her head back and laughed to think that she had fooled no one.

In spite of the way she had avoided his phone call, she was as real and uncontrived as he'd always known her to be. She was definitely her own person, neatly wrapped around some inner core. She was emotional, vulnerable, passionately loyal to her ideals. Something stronger than pride had driven her here today when the wounds were still so fresh between them. It was courage, he knew. Courage in spite of the odds. It was that about her which thrilled him beyond everything else, and which prompted him to ask a little too eagerly, "Would you like to stay for lunch?"

Catherine's dark eyes were sparkling bright and there was still a trace of laughter in her voice when she answered, "Okay."

"Why don't you go on up to the house while I finish here? You can wash up before we eat. Millie can show you where the bathroom is."

The unappreciating look she gave him and the saucy bounce to her gait as she walked off told him that she already knew where it was.

She had certainly been in this house enough times in the past to know where the bathroom was. Nevertheless, Catherine politely asked the housekeeper if she could use the bathroom, and accepted with thanks the woman's directions to the second floor.

She knew that the bathroom was through another room and made her way to it. She did not, however, anticipate that behind the door would be Cal's bedroom. As she recalled, his room used to be down the hall. Yet, when she opened the door and peered inside, there was little doubt that this was his room.

The room baked in the quiet heat of the day. Myriad particles danced in the rays of sunlight that streamed through the open window. The furnishings had changed over the years, yet as Catherine's eyes moved about the room, she also noticed that Cal's preference for simple things was still the same. A simple oak dresser stood against one wall. The bed was spread with clean white sheets. An old Hudson's Bay blanket served as a rug.

Catherine recognized at once the colorful blanket with its traditional points woven into the wool as the one that used to hang on the wall in Cal's father's study. The blanket brimmed with history. It had come from the Hudson Bay store at Frog Lake where, on an April day in 1885, a band of Cree Indians attacked, killing, looting and taking prisoners. The Canadian militia had been called out to suppress the armed revolt, but not before one of the survivors of the attack had escaped into the forest wearing nothing but this very blanket.

Touched off by the sight of the familiar object, the memories came flooding back. Memories of this house, of Pitchfork, of the constantly-blue Albertan sky froze Catherine on the threshold, just shy of entering. She had no idea how long she stood, lost in remembering, but she gradually became aware of a presence behind her. She didn't have to hear him approach, nor hear his voice, low and gently mocking, to know he was there.

"Homey, isn't it?"

She answered simply, "It's you."

He moved past her into the room. "Remember that old blanket?" He pointed to it as he strode toward the bathroom.

It was as if he knew she'd been thinking about it. It used to be like that between them, she recalled.

Sometimes it was scary the way they'd known each other's thoughts. "It looks good there," she said.

He disappeared into the bathroom without bothering to close the door behind him, his voice calling, "Thanks. I like it there, too. I figured, if it survived an Indian attack, it wouldn't hurt to use it as a rug."

She heard the sound of water splashing in the sink. He emerged a few minutes later, wiping his face on a towel and smelling faintly of Ivory soap. "Of course, it doesn't get walked on much. With the hours I keep, I'm lucky if I make it to bed by midnight. Breeding season's always rough. I don't mind telling you, I'm bushed." He looked at Catherine, who was still standing in the doorway, and asked, "Haven't you washed up yet?"

Was it possible, she was wondering as she watched him, that he was unaware of the impact a clean-smelling, bare-chested man had on a woman? Or was it that he knew precisely what he was doing? Catherine cleared her throat of the lump caused by the blatant distraction of his near nakedness and replied, "No, I haven't."

"What are you waiting for?"

"For you to get out of the bathroom."

"Well, I'm out."

From where she stood the doorway to the bathroom could well have been ten miles away, and standing smack in the middle of her path was a dangerously sexy man. Catherine swallowed hard and willed her feet to move.

He was waiting for her when she got there, as she knew he would be. Who was kidding whom? It was his way of making her come to him and they both knew it.

One second he was standing there, the next his body was against hers, his mouth and his hands everywhere.

It was as if these last few days converged upon this moment. Unnerved by the force of Cal's kiss, Catherine moaned defenselessly. Pleasure coursed through her. She lifted her arms, surrendering to its throbbing rhythm.

She felt herself backed slowly against the wall and pinned there. If there was any hesitation or doubt as to what she was getting herself into, it vanished the instant his hot, wet mouth found the tip of her breast through the fabric of her T-shirt.

His lovemaking bore little resemblance to the tender coupling of the other night. His lips sucked greedily at the smooth white flesh of her throat as his hands worked roughly to undress her. He pulled the clothes off her as he used his strength to slide her slowly down the wall. When she was naked beneath him, atop the Hudson's Bay blanket on the floor, he buried his fingers in the cool, rich softness of her hair and forced her head back.

He looked deeply into her brown eyes and in a hoarse voice he said, "There'll be no more evasions between us, Cathy. You're swollen with wanting, just like me."

Her lips curved slightly with all the words she wanted to say but was afraid to. "You arrogant bastard," she said. "Making me want you like this. Telling me what *you* want and then making me want it, too."

He silenced her with a hard kiss and then whispered against her mouth, "I don't care what you say as long as I can have you like this."

Not a word about love or caring, she noticed, and yet there was something distinctly thrilling in his lust. It heightened her own sexual appetite to the point of bursting. Without thinking, she nudged him onto his back and rolled on top of him. She scattered light butterfly kisses on his forehead, his nose, his eyelids, and his chin. Her mouth was hot and sweetly scented when it covered his in a long kiss while her eager hands found the zipper of his jeans.

Cal lay like a gathering storm. The heat of her breath against his skin, the flick of her teasing tongue between his lips, the press of her breasts against his chest all drove him wild with passion. But when she took his face in her hands and kissed the scar on his cheek, it drove him clear over the edge.

She had discovered for the first time the other night just how big and strong he was when fully aroused, but the tenderness with which he'd loved her had made it easy. There was no such gentleness about him now, however, as he poured into her with hard, deep thrusts that pushed her head up against the wall. There was a wildness about him, a dangerous and exciting edge to his forceful lovemaking as his hands cupped her from beneath and he lifted her to him, higher, deeper, until his body shuddered with one final thrust.

Catherine's own body arched in answer as wave upon wave of passion washed over her, and were it not for his arms that grasped her close, she was sure she would have drowned in pleasure.

Pleasure, she told herself afterwards when she got up from the floor and reached for her clothes. There was no denying the incredible pleasure they derived from each other's bodies. Yet, a part of Catherine yearned for something far more with this man, something seemingly forbidden by events of the past, and yet inescapably right.

As she dressed, she thought of her marriage and the constant need she'd had to validate herself within it. The high-powered world of business and politics, in which she'd served merely as an adornment to a ambitious man, was as foreign as the moon to the young woman who preferred to run barefoot through the tall grass of the Canadian foothills. Of all the things surrounding her, she had learned to take special comfort in the steel and glass skyscrapers, for in their height and strength she was reminded of the tall peaks she used to look at from her grandfather's front porch.

Her thoughts came full circle back to the moment, to Cal, and to the last fifteen minutes with him on the floor that had thrilled her more than anything else in the last ten years. He'd never seemed to have any problem accepting her for who she was. Even now, in spite of the triumphant little smile on his face as he tugged on his jeans and pulled a fresh T-shirt over his head, she sensed that he was not judging her.

"What's for lunch?" she asked.

"What else?" he said, green eyes sparkling. "That melt-in-your-mouth smoothness of Alberta sweet-grass-fed-and-grain-finished steak."

"Walker bred, no doubt."

His grin widened as he boasted, "Prepare yourself for the best meal you'll ever have."

"Really? Remind me to invite you over for dinner some time when we're having roast lamb." She disappeared into the bathroom and closed the door behind her.

Catherine had to admit that it was the best steak she'd ever eaten, cooked to rare perfection on the barbecue by Millie, Cal's housekeeper. The woman had done her best to hide a slightly amused smile when they'd come downstairs together. Cal had mumbled something about showing Catherine the old Hudson's Bay blanket, making Catherine blush with embarrassment.

During the meal they talked of things that hardly mattered, neither mentioning the way they'd both been tricked, each treading cautiously to avoid breaking the fragile thread between them. Cal talked of the ranch and of the changes he'd made since he'd been back, avoiding the event that had sent him away in the first place, and the lonely years in between. Catherine spoke of her grandfather and the crumbling little sheep ranch she had inherited from him, and of the responsibility she felt to keep it going.

"I wonder what Angus would say if he could see it now," she said with a dismal sigh.

"If Angus were here," said Cal, "he'd tell you that if you don't take a chance, you don't stand a chance."

She looked at him curiously. "How do you know he'd say something like that?"

"Because he said it to me once."

He didn't bother to explain that it was the day he'd driven by the old Scotsman's place to tell him he was leaving. He'd had a few days since Ellis Randolph's visit for his violent rage to subside, and then a kind of numbness had set in. He'd said nothing about the bribe, nor his real reasons for leaving Pitchfork. There had been no sense talking about it, especially when Angus began to ramble on about taking chances. Hell, he'd taken the biggest chance of all only to lose in the end.

The hour went swiftly. Soon, their coffee cups were empty and it was suddenly time to leave.

Millie emerged from the kitchen to clear the table, glancing now and again at Catherine and Cal as she did. She'd never seen two people just sit there like that without talking and yet saying so much with their eyes. Her cheeks reddened at what she read in their gazes. Feeling like an intruder, even though they seemed truly oblivious to her presence, she quickly disappeared from the room.

Cal pushed his chair back and stood up. He stood beside her and looked down at her. His voice was softly urging. "Let's go upstairs."

Catherine felt pinned to her seat beneath the weight of Cal's stare, trapped by the sight of the raw hunger in his eyes. She knew she should rise. She wanted to, but she couldn't. It was all happening too fast. So what if she *had* come over here this afternoon to be with him, and so what if they both knew it? Those summers with him, and the long, lonely years without, could not be erased with one single afternoon of uninhibited pleasure. And yet, until that first night in his arms, she'd never felt anything like it.

The tenderness of the night at her place, when he'd held her and helped ease her fears, and the forceful, almost brutal, way he'd taken her in his bedroom each thrilled her in its way. Each time she'd felt as if it were her very first time.

Her gaze came up slowly to meet his. Her eyes were dark, almost black, and inviting. She rose from her seat and stood before him, cheeks faintly blushed. The air grew dangerously warm as they stood mere inches apart without touching.

When he took her hand to lead the way upstairs, she didn't pull back. When her clothes lay atop his in a puddle on the floor, she didn't resist. The sheets smelled crisp and clean, and the cool cotton percale felt good against her heated flesh. She was beyond thought, oblivious to what tomorrow would bring.

All that mattered was the hard, flat belly pressing against hers. The thick, sculptured muscles of the arms that held her close. The rasp of a calloused palm across her breast. The slow, sensual thrusting of his body taking her to the brink of madness.

When the final moment came, Catherine would have screamed except that Cal's mouth covered hers. She clung to him, her body going rigid, and then limp as she collapsed in his arms.

There were no words afterwards to describe what she was feeling. No man had ever loved her like that, and to have experienced that kind of passion with the man she'd wanted and desired and craved for ten long years was like a fantasy come true.

She should have been deliriously happy, but she wasn't, not when a small voice at the back of her mind kept asking what physical desire had to do with love.

"What's the matter?" he asked. "Regrets?"

She stirred in his embrace, nestling closer to him. "No, no regrets. You were . . . wonderful."

He caught her under the chin with the tip of his forefinger and guided her face toward his. "I've dreamed of you this way," he whispered. "Since you came back, you've been driving me mad. The smell of you. The way you walk. The way you toss your head back to get the hair out of your eyes. You turn me on, Cathy. You know you do. But then, I was always a sucker for those big brown eyes."

He bent his head to nuzzle the sensitive flesh beneath her breast and gave each rosy peak a long, deep kiss. "These are real nice, too."

There were a million things she wanted to ask him. Like, what about love? Did he still love her? But she didn't ask, too afraid of the answer she would hear.

Though much about him was familiar, he was still very much a stranger to her. Until only a few nights ago his beautiful naked body had been an unknown to her as well. It had been dark that first time, too dark to really see him. And earlier today, in the heated rush of their lovemaking, she'd had little time to think, much less take in his physical attributes. But now, with the late afternoon sunlight filling the room, Catherine gazed fully and plainly upon his nakedness.

There was a scar on his right forearm. She ran her fingertips across it.

"Caught on a nail fixing the barn," he murmured, eyes closed.

She touched the two-inch scar on his lower abdomen.

"Appendix."

She touched a jagged line on his calf.

"Fell off a horse."

He was feeling relaxed and unguarded as her fingers gently explored, until he felt her touch at his cheek, and suddenly everything inside of him went rigid.

Catherine's voice was soft and inquisitive, a mere

breath against his skin as she quietly ventured, "And this?"

His eyes came slowly open. The scar that slashed across his cheek began to grow warmer and throb. He opened his mouth to speak but no words emerged. That was something he just couldn't talk about. And besides, did she really want to know the part she had played in putting the indelible mark on his cheek?

"Let's just say, I'll be damned if I ever go near another oil rig again."

He gave her no time to question him further when he rolled on top of her, pinning her to the mattress with his weight and kissing her breath away.

Catherine shuddered at the renewed passion she felt building within him, and responded in kind with her own urgent need. And yet, except for some cryptic mumbling about an oil rig, she did not fail to notice that he hadn't answered the question.

NINE

During the first ten years of the twentieth century, a flood of settlers poured into the territory by way of the new Canadian Pacific Railway, spurred on by the government's promise of homestead land for ten dollars per quarter section. Among the immigrants was Angus Coleman, his parents, and siblings.

When the Dingman Number One well yielded oil at Turner Valley, eleven-year-old Angus was seized with the desire to be an oilman. It was a dream hard fought for but lost in the long run.

At the age of fifteen Angus Coleman ran away from home and got himself hired onto his first drilling crew by lying about his age. When Alberta's first oil refinery opened in Calgary a few years later, he was one of the first, and youngest, to be employed.

But Angus Coleman wasn't suited to working for others. His wife, Elizabeth, called the irascible nature that had gotten him fired from many jobs his finest point and his worst. In the 1930s, when his luck in the oil industry didn't pan out, he found an outlet for his restless energy by joining a group of pioneering bush pilots, among them several World War I flying aces, and helped make aviation history in his primitive aircraft by linking the city of Edmonton with the far north.

In 1947, when that first well around Edmonton blew black for days, when everyone else plunged headlong into the rush of black gold, Angus Coleman took the money he earned from flying and turned his back on it all. He bought some land, one hundred head of sheep, and went into business for himself over the sharp objections of his new neighbors, the Walkers.

Over the ensuing years, he lost Elizabeth to pneumonia during a bad winter, his daughter, Mary, to a son-in-law he disliked, and his granddaughter, Catherine, to a broken heart. His one and only attempt to fulfill his childhood dream had failed when the well on the northeast quarter came up dry. In the end, all that was left was the pesky little sheep ranch in the foothills of the Rockies.

It was all there in the old trunk, one man's history told through the yellowed pages of the love letters to her grandmother, a journal filled with random entries and afterthoughts, old flying reports, a haphazardly kept business ledger filled with notations and doodlings in the margins.

It was Labor Day weekend. Ben and Gertie had gone to Gertie's folks in Red Deer. Catherine had graciously declined Gertie's invitation to join them. The prospect of three days to herself was too hard for her to pass up. After assuring Gertie that she would eat three square meals a day, and convincing

Ben that she, Sam, and Bing could get the sheep in on their own, she had waved good-bye from the porch as they drove off in the pickup truck.

After doing her chores, she had saddled Bing and gone for a ride. Later, with Sam's help she got the sheep in. There wasn't much to do after that, and it had been too early for dinner, so she read a little with her legs stretched out on the sofa. It was a mixture of boredom and curiosity that made her eventually put the book aside and wander upstairs.

The air in the low-beamed attic was hot and stale as Catherine knelt before the old steamer trunk, sifting carefully through the fragile contents. She gingerly lifted out the packet of letters bound with a faded blue ribbon and read the words of the love-struck young man for beautiful Elizabeth McLeod, the girl he married and obviously adored for more than fifty years. The flying reports reverberated with the freedom he found in the air. The random journal entries coincided with milestones along the way, such as the birth of his daughter, Mary, which had forced him to quit flying and stay closer to home.

Strangely, there was not a single mention, not one word of the failed attempt to drill his own well. Catherine thought it sad. Why, if anyone other than she were looking through the trunk, they would never have known of the venture, nor of the courage it had taken to pursue the dream, nor what it had cost in pride for Angus to go to his son-in-law for a loan to finance the project, nor of the rejection.

But Catherine knew. She'd seen it in the look of bitter disappointment on her grandfather's face when he walked in the door after having gone to see her father for the loan. She'd heard it in the disillusioned burr of his voice.

Strangely, however, Catherine's memories of her grandfather were not of the bad times, but of the good, of the lilting Scottish brogue and the dancing blue eyes. And even if the record of his drilling venture was lost now to everything except her memory, there was enough nostalgia in the old trunk to warm her heart and make her lose track of the time.

Beyond the small window at the far end of the sloping attic walls, the sun sank lower in the sky, but Catherine didn't notice. She was engrossed in one of the many letters she had penned to her grandfather, feeling touched to the point of tears to find that he had saved each and every one.

The sound of a creaking timber brought her head up. She was surprised to see the approach of twilight in the eerie kind of light, dust-filled and misty, beyond the window. She had never cared for this time of day, hovering as it did somewhere between day and night, not quite one, but not quite the other. If she were downstairs, she'd be pulling down the shades and turning on lights, and in a short time the state of limbo would pass and it would be night. Up here in the attic, however, there was no shade to be pulled over the small, paned window. Nothing to blot out that unexplained feeling of fear that invariably pervaded her at times like this, when she was alone at this time of day.

The creaking sounds from the far end of the room didn't help Catherine's growing sense of apprehension, but when she realized that it was the creaking of the attic stairs, she grew scared.

Catherine froze at the unmistakable sound of footsteps coming up the stairs. Who was it? Her first thought was that it was Cal, and she felt her pulse quicken. But that wasn't Cal's frame that passed through the doorway and stood now in silhouette against the dim light. Catherine's heart began to beat faster.

The figure moved forward, seeming to come right out of the light toward her. Above the rapid pounding of fear at her temples, she heard the tap, tap of his footsteps on the floorboards. She was seized by an irrational urge to duck and hide behind the trunk, but he'd already seen her. There was nothing she could do except remain where she was as the figure came closer.

It wasn't until he was standing over her and she was looking up at him from the dusty floor that Catherine's fear subsided. Nevertheless, she felt distinct discomfort at Drew Devlin's presence.

"No one answered when I knocked," he said. "The door was open so I came in. I hope you don't mind."

Mind? Why should she mind? Because he'd scared her half to death? Because there was something about him that she didn't like? Her father had cautioned her to trust no one. Her grandfather, however, had taught her not to judge.

"Of course not," she said, smiling up at him. "You did startle me, though. I wasn't expecting company."

"Where is everyone?" he asked.

"*Everyone* is my foreman Ben and his wife, Gertie, and they're away for the holiday weekend. I'm surprised to see you here," she added. "I thought you were away for the holiday also."

"I was," he said. "I went fishing at Killdeer Lake. Those big-mouth bass are really biting."

"What brought you back? No emergencies, I hope."

"Not at all," he replied. "It was just time to return."

If Catherine thought it was strange that he would go away for the holiday and return prematurely for no apparent reason, she kept it to herself. And then an alarming thought occurred to her. Did it have something to do with her sheep? Had he come to warn her of an epidemic?

"That sheep you examined for me," she said. "The one you autopsied? What precisely was the cause of death?"

"I gave that information to your foreman," said Devlin. "Didn't he tell you I called?"

"Yes, of course, he did. But I'd like to hear it again, if you don't mind."

Devlin repeated for her what he had told her foreman, feeling a little put out by her questioning. Her skepticism annoyed him. She didn't want to hear it again, he thought, she wanted to hear it for herself.

An awkward silence passed between them, which Devlin broke when he nodded toward the trunk, and said, "Find anything good in there?"

Catherine had forgotten all about the trunk and the letter that was still in her hand. She folded it up and slipped it back beneath the ribbon. "Nothing much," she said as she put the packet back in the trunk.

"I hear your grandfather was quite a character," said Devlin. "Who knows what kinds of things you might discover when you begin to look? You know, deeds, old records, reports, letters. Say, didn't he once even drill for oil?''

She figured he had learned about that from his uncle, and answered, ''He tried, but the well dried up.''

''That's too bad. Still, he must have left records. Geologists' reports, things like that.''

She had thought the same thing until she'd looked in the trunk and discovered otherwise. ''If he did, it's not here.''

Closing the lid on the trunk, she got to her feet. ''Can I get you something cold to drink? If I know Gertie, there's a pitcher of lemonade in the refrigerator.''

''Thanks, I could use it. It's hotter than hell up here.''

Yes, she had noticed the way he'd begun to sweat, the gradual moistening of his collar as he stood there, the tiny beads of wetness that formed at his forehead and on his upper lip. All in spite of the fact that the sun had practically disappeared from the sky and the air had cooled considerably, prompting Catherine to wonder if it was something else that was making him sweat.

''By the way,'' she said to him from over her shoulder as she led the way down the narrow staircase, ''you never said what brought you out here today. You don't have bad news for me, do you?''

He watched her as she walked in front of him to the kitchen. She was wearing shorts that exposed long, tanned legs, and a tank top that showed taut shoulders and the firm muscles of her back. He found himself strangely unaroused. Beautiful women didn't impress him. If anything did, it was wealth. Maybe that's why he felt uncomfortable being here. The

Coleman place, with its ramshackled buildings and downtrodden appearance, gave him the creeps. The place should have gone out of business years ago, but it hadn't. It seemed to survive out of pure spite.

"I won't know that until I can look at more animals," he said. "That's why it's imperative that you immediately bring me any others you find. You haven't found any others, have you?"

As she poured him a glass of lemonade, Catherine thought guiltily of the specimen she'd taken to Pitchfork. She didn't look at him as she handed him the glass and lied, "No, I haven't.

"Good. Be sure and phone me if you do."

"Sure thing," she said as she walked him to the door. "Thank you for driving out here today."

"No problem. When I got the message that you had called, I thought you might be worried."

"That was kind of you," she said, softening a little toward him.

Maybe he did care after all. It was odd, but she sometimes got the impression that he wasn't much interested in what he was doing. She sensed no passion about the man. It was as if his work was just a means to an end, although what that end was she couldn't guess. She knew it was crazy. She hardly knew the man well enough to make a judgment like that. Rather, it was something she sensed about him that made her eager to see him leave.

Why, he doesn't like being here, Catherine thought with a shock as she watched the way his eyes moved over the surroundings. A look of contempt swept like a dark wind across his face, gone in the next instant when he climbed into his fancy car, flashed her a smile, and drove off.

She watched from the porch as his red tail lights disappeared into the growing darkness. She was relieved that he hadn't come bearing bad news, and she supposed that it had been nice of him to drive all the way out here when he could just as easily have telephoned. Still, she knew no more than she did before. One sheep was dead from sheep tick and countless others were missing. Where were they disappearing to? Had they, too, died after being bitten, only to wind up as carrion for the night scavengers?

The unanswered questions plagued Catherine through a lonely, brooding dinner, after which she retired early. She tried reading for a while, but her eyelids soon drooped and she fell asleep with the book open across her chest.

She had no idea how long she'd been sleeping, when her eyes popped open to total darkness. Something had awakened her as surely as a rough hand on her shoulder. She sat bolt upright in bed. She thought at first that she was still dreaming, but when she heard the pounding on the front door, she knew what had awakened her. She was out of bed and slipping into her robe all in one motion. Her bare feet carried her quickly downstairs to answer the door.

She expected to see Ben and Gertie standing there, having returned early for some reason. No doubt Gertie would be surprised, and Ben would be angry, to find the door locked. After the easy way in which Drew Devlin had gained entry this afternoon, Catherine had locked the door, planning to unlock it later, and simply forgetting to.

A quick glance at the clock on the mantle as she hurried through the living room, revealed that it was past midnight. What on earth had made them come back in the middle of the night?

But when Catherine opened the door, it was neither Gertie's round face nor Ben's angular one that greeted her. Instead, it was Cal's scarred handsomeness that looked back at her through the mesh of the screen door.

"Cal! Come in."

The hinges squeaked as she pushed the screen door open for him to step through. She went to turn on the lamp. The dim yellow light filled the room with a warm glow that was reflected on her cheeks when she returned to him.

"What are you doing here?"

It was obvious from the huskiness in her voice that he had awakened her. She looked more beautiful in disarray than most women looked after an hour of making up, and for several moments he stared at her without answering, as a predictable longing churned inside of him.

She was so near to him that he had merely to put his hand out to part the folds of her robe. It would have been so easy to wind his arm around her small waist and pull her down onto the sofa. And she would have let him, he knew she would, just as she had that first time and after that. The first time had been out of need. The second out of pure pent-up lust. Would there ever come a time when it would be out of love? Cal wondered bitterly.

Cal had always sensed that his attraction to Cathy Coleman was part of a larger, more curious ache. He felt touched somewhere deep inside not only by her beauty, but by the essence of her. Around her, he'd always felt slightly crazy. There was something amazingly alluring about her, something that he sensed even now could grow and obsess him. The truth was that he'd never stopped loving her.

Cal forced his disquieting thoughts aside and said, "I drove into Edmonton today on business. I didn't get home until late. This was waiting for me when I got there."

It was then that she noticed the manila envelope, which had been dangling unnoticed from his hand and which he now held out to her.

She knew immediately what it was. "You could have phoned me. You didn't have to drive over at this hour."

He had wrestled with himself over how he would tell her. Several times he had picked up the phone to call her, but had felt too much like a coward and had hung up without dialing. She'd had the courage to come to him for help. The least he could do was break the news to her in person.

"It's bad news, Cathy."

Her face went pale. She let out a desperate little sigh and muttered, "Sheep tick."

She looked so damned vulnerable standing there wearing nothing but a robe and a worried expression. He hated being the one to tell her. "No, not sheep tick. Poison."

Catherine's dark eyes stared back at him with a blank expression that slowly filled with realizaton, and then with suspicion. "Poison?" she echoed. "That's ridiculous. Where would any of my sheep come in contact with poison?"

"At Pitchfork, we sometimes use it to get rid of barn rats. Why don't you ask your foreman what he does with his."

Catherine let out a loud breath of frustration and pleaded, "Cal, would you please lay off Ben?"

"Did you ever ask him about the brake fluid?" he persisted.

"That was . . . nothing. An accident, that's all." She would die before she admitted to him that she had never confronted Ben about the brake fluid. Didn't she have enough troubles without opening up that can of worms?

Catherine went to the sofa and slumped down onto it. She was unaware that the folds of her robe had slipped open over her long, bronzed legs, oblivious to the sight she presented dressed in next to nothing, having forgotten for the time being about the man who stood quietly watching.

Poison. She repeated the word over and over again in her mind, as if by repetition it would make some sense.

The cushions sagged when Cal sat down beside her. Placing a hand gently on her shoulder, he drew her away from the thoughts that were plainly written on her face.

"Look, Cathy, maybe it's an isolated incident."

"And if it's not?"

He had no answer.

She shrugged away from him and rose. Back and forth she paced, wringing her hands with worry. "I don't understand it," she exclaimed. "Why would anyone want to poison my sheep? What do they want?"

"Well," said Cal from the sofa, "assuming that someone *is* trying to poison your sheep, which we don't know for certain, maybe it's to see you go under."

"I'm no threat to anyone else's business," she insisted.

"Well then, maybe they want the place for themselves."

She shot him a severely-doubting look. "I can barely keep this place going. I'm practically bankrupt!"

"Hey, Cathy, I didn't say I had all the answers," he protested. "But you asked me why anyone would want to poison your sheep, and I've just given you two reasons."

"I'm sorry, Cal. I guess I've just been on edge lately. And hysterics certainly won't help."

He got up and went to her and turned her gently around to face him. "You know something? Even on the verge of hysterics, you're beautiful."

She managed a halfhearted smile up at him. "You were always a charmer."

He returned the smile. "With you, it always came easy."

The smile faded from her face and those chocolate-brown eyes looked up at him fearfully. "Cal, there's nothing here except a couple hundred head of sheep."

"I know, Cathy. It beats the hell out of me, too."

Catherine ran her fingers through her hair, sweeping the chestnut locks away from her face and muttering, "Great. So now what do I do?"

"You wait."

"For what? For someone to poison the rest of my sheep?"

There was a bitter ring to her tone when she turned away and said, "I can give up."

"What!" He grasped her sharply by the arm and spun her around. "You don't mean that."

"Why not?" she complained. "Things haven't gone right for the last ten years, why should it be any different now?"

"That doesn't sound like you, Cathy," said Cal, his fingers tightening around her upper arm for emphasis.

"You think you know me so well?" The challenge was as blatant in her icy tone as in the upward tilt of her chin.

"You're damned right I do," he answered in a low, tense voice that told her not to argue. "For ten years I didn't think I knew you at all. Then it turns out that what I thought you were guilty of never happened. That's a laugh, isn't it? I knew you just as well during those years as I ever did, only I didn't realize it. And you know what, Cathy? You're no different than you used to be. The only difference is that you were a girl then and you're a woman now, but you're just as strong-willed as you ever were. And reckless? Christ, Cathy, the way you rush headlong into things? And you know what else? You're just like him. Just as proud and stubborn as that old Scotsman."

He drew her closer as he spoke, his fingers like a vice around her arm. "And God help me, but you're just as beautiful as you ever were."

She expected to be drawn none too gently into his arms and kissed with all the fury she saw simmering in those green eyes, and was thrown a curve when he released her and turned away with a look of disgust on his face, as if he hated himself for what he was feeling.

He walked to the door, saying without looking at

her, "Hell, Cathy, you have to stand for something, or you'll fall for anything."

Grimly, she noted, "That sounds like something my grandfather would say."

"As a matter-of-fact, he did say it, in an argument he had once with my father. He drove over to Pitchfork in that old VW, mad as hell and hollering about Pitchfork cattle being on his land. My father told him if he didn't like it, to sell his place and leave. Angus got all red in the face. I'd just come out of the barn and saw him. For a minute I thought maybe he was going to explode, but he didn't. He got that look on his face—you know the look I mean—and said to my father, 'You gotta stand for something or you'll fall for anything.' I think if Angus were here now he'd tell you the same thing, Cathy."

She trailed after him in her bare feet, outside into the still summer night. Ribbons of moonlight fell across her face as she stood at the porch railing for several minutes just staring out into the darkness.

"You're right, of course," she said at length. "Self-pity isn't my style. Neither is giving up."

From behind her she heard him mutter, "I wonder."

"What?"

"Just a thought. When Angus tried drilling for oil, why'd he stop?"

"No oil, I guess. Why?"

"You don't know for sure?"

"Well, no, he never said. It was something he didn't talk about."

"I can understand that. But what if he stopped for a different reason?"

"Like what?"

"Like maybe he ran out of money."

"So what if he did? What does that have to do with anything?"

Cal shrugged and ventured, "Who knows? Maybe there's still oil under your land. Man, wouldn't that be something?"

Sourly, she said, "We'll never know. There aren't any drilling reports. I've looked. And I can't afford to hire a geologist to find out."

"Cathy, if you need the money, I could—"

"No!"

The force of her reply startled Catherine as much as it did Cal. She hadn't meant to sound as if she were jumping all over him, but she wasn't a charity case, damn it.

"That won't be necessary, Cal. Thank you."

He knew it was her stubborn pride that was doing the talking. If she hadn't taken money from a wealthy ex-husband, he should have known she wouldn't take any from him either.

"Have it your way, Cath. Just remember, the offer's there if you need it."

He walked across the porch and down the steps and headed for his pickup in that long and languid stride that had always reminded her of a cat's.

After he had gone, Catherine lay awake in bed feeling as if she had entered the uncharted territory of the *Twilight Zone*. Her mind was traveling faster than the speed of light, making it impossible for her to sleep. Oil beneath her land? It was preposterous. She had about as much chance of there being oil beneath her land as she had of winning the lottery. Geologists' reports would have proved once and for all that it was oil Angus had run out of, and not money as Cal had suggested. But without the existence of drilling reports, it was all beside the point.

And yet, in order for Angus to have approached her father for the money to finance his drilling venture, wouldn't he had to have produced geologists' reports to prove there was oil? Catherine had always assumed her father turned Angus down because the reports had not been convincing, but maybe there'd been another reason. A reason no one would ever know.

TEN

In the days following summer's end there was a discernible tension in the autumn air as Catherine more and more found herself at odds with Ben over matters pertaining to the daily running of the ranch.

They hadn't discovered any more sheep missing in the last few weeks, thus relieving Catherine of the task of telling about the findings of the Pitchfork vet. The supposedly different findings from the two veterinarians were sure to spark a confrontation with Ben that she wished to avoid. There was too much work to be done to keep the place going for them to be arguing like children.

Cal called a couple of times to find out if anything new had developed and they wound up talking for more than an hour of nothing in particular, the way they used to do. These days things were hectic at Pitchfork as he prepared for winter, and he had managed to find the time to drive over only once to see her. It had been late one evening when Catherine had been sitting on the porch talking with Gertie. The sight of his pickup truck coming up the road had caused a familiar lurch of her heart.

The distraction he caused was always a painful one for Catherine, for it was an ever-constant reminder of the way things used to be between them. And even though a part of her was relieved that he'd been too busy to drive over again, she found herself constantly looking over her shoulder for a sight of his pickup coming up the road.

The screen door creaked open and Gertie appeared on the porch, wiping her hands on her apron. "We've got more than enough for dinner," she said. "Why don't you invite him over?"

Catherine looked up at her from where she was sitting on the top step of the porch, taking a break from her work. "Invite who over?"

"Why, that nice Mister Walker, of course. The one you were just thinking about."

Catherine's cheeks colored at the ease with which Gertie read her thoughts. Was it her imagination, or had Gertie mentioned Cal's name now several times since that night they'd been sitting on the porch and he had showed up? Catherine had noticed the way Gertie had slipped quietly inside to leave them alone. Why was Gertie being so gracious to Cal Walker when it was obvious that her husband disapproved of him?

She looked up into the housekeeper's friendly eyes and said, "Oh? It's that nice Mister Walker now, is it?"

The woman shrugged her ample shoulders and replied, "I never said I didn't like him. I just said he looked lonely to me."

"In any case," said Catherine, "I don't think your husband would care for Cal Walker at the same dinner table."

"Oh, Ben don't mean anything. Besides, I can always get around him. All I mean is, if you want to invite him for dinner, don't let us stop you."

"What makes you think I would want to invite Cal Walker over for dinner?" Catherine asked.

Candidly, the woman replied, "I'm not blind, Catherine. For one thing, I saw the way you two looked at each other the other night. For another, you're blushing."

Catherine got up and dusted off the seat of her jeans. "Thanks, Gertie, but I'm sure Cal's busy. Just like I am." She started down the steps. "Back to work."

"You should take a break," said Gertie. "You've been working too hard."

"Can't stop now, Gertie, or we'll all be out of jobs. Besides, what on earth would I do with myself if I didn't work? I'd be bored out of my mind."

"Good heavens! With all that beautiful scenery out there and that gorgeous hunk of man over at Pitchfork?"

"Gertie, if I didn't know any better, I'd say you were playing matchmaker."

"And I'd say the match was made a long time ago."

Catherine lowered her eyes at the unexpected remark. "A memory, Gertie, that's all it is. Just like the ones in that old trunk in the attic. A memory that has nothing to do with today."

The woman sighed with mild frustration. "But Catherine, memories just like the ones in the trunk in the attic and the carton in the shearing shed link us to the present."

How could she explain to this kindhearted woman how desperately she wished things between her and Cal could be the same? She looked at her imploringly and whispered, "You don't know."

Gertie smiled tenderly. "I know what it's like to love a man."

From the look in the other woman's eyes, Catherine knew it was useless to deny it. "Sometimes love doesn't feel like it should."

"He's a good man, Catherine."

"Yes," she admitted. "Cal's a good man."

"No," said Gertie. "I meant my Ben."

As Catherine headed back to work, she thought about how difficult it must be for Gertie, for surely the woman sensed the tension between Ben and herself. Gertie had spoken of love. Maybe Gertie loved her husband too much to see his faults, but Catherine didn't view Ben McFarland in quite the same light.

Fresh in her mind was the accident on the lonely road from Edmonton and the matter of the brake fluid that had been allowed to get down too low. In addition to that, some of her sheep were missing, one had been poisoned, and she had one disgruntled foreman on her hands. Was it all just a coincidence? Or was there a connection? She had no reason to suspect Ben McFarland guilty of anything more than negligence and a belligerent disposition. Still, she could not help but wonder.

Overgrown with dust and memories, the shearing shed was silent when Catherine entered. In a corner, set behind the shearing tools and a rusty old generator that hadn't worked in years, she found the cardboard carton that Gertie had unwittingly alluded to. It wasn't very heavy when she pulled it out into the open, making Catherine think she was wasting her time.

After the funeral Catherine had given some of her grandfather's things away and packed up most of the rest of his belongings before returning to Boston. She recalled now asking Gertie to pack up whatever was left when she'd hired the McFarlands.

There were no love letters inside, no notebooks filled with personal remembrances. Nevertheless, what Catherine found when she opened the box shook her up.

There was Angus's pipe, the one always burning with sweet-smelling tobacco. She picked it up and held it to her nose. Yes, that was it, she thought fondly, that was the smell she remembered so well.

She found the old bone-handle pocket knife he used to whittle with. The shaving cup and brush that had sat like a permanent fixture on the bathroom shelf. The leather-bound Bible he'd kept by the bed and read every night before going to sleep. The gold pocket watch and fob her grandmother had given him one Christmas.

The memories sprang from every object Catherine touched and she found herself missing him desperately. But it wasn't until she discovered the woolen vest he used to wear on chilly winter nights that she felt the tears begin to well.

She drew it close to her face and breathed in deeply, hoping to catch a hint of him, but the years had dulled the scent and all that remained was the faint must of time. She lowered the vest and was about to put it back into the box when something slipped out of the pocket.

A yellowed envelope fluttered into her lap. Inside it she found a letter addressed to "Dear Angus". The vest and all of the other objects were momentarily forgotten as Catherine read the letter that thanked her grandfather for the offer, but sadly declined. It made reference to a loan and expressed regret that there wasn't more to lend. It was signed simply, "Your friend, Andrew."

Catherine stared at the letter. Andrew? And then it hit her. Of course! Andrew Devlin, the veterinarian. She smiled. She had always liked old Doc Devlin. He and Angus had been friends for as long as she could remember. They had argued constantly and never agreed on a thing, but she knew there had been a wealth of mutual admiration and respect bonding the two Scotsmen.

The letter raised new questions in Catherine's mind. What offer had the sheepman made to the veterinarian? And what had the loan been for? A gradual realization came upon her, and even though she had no proof on which to base her assumptions, she suddenly knew what it was all about.

There was no doubt in Catherine's mind that her grandfather had offered Andrew Devlin a partnership in the oil well. For a reason she would never know the offer had been reluctantly turned down. Perhaps it didn't matter why. What was important was that she now knew where her grandfather had obtained the money to finance his venture. Surely, that was the loan referred to in the letter. And it made sense, too. With the ranch mortgaged to the hilt, and having been turned down by his son-in-law, where else would Angus have gone other than to his old friend?

Catherine had always assumed that her grandfather had abandoned his well because there was no oil, but maybe Cal was right. Maybe he'd stopped drilling because he simply ran out of money. Hadn't Doc Devlin expressed his regret over not having more money to lend? Of course, that was it!

Her hopes were beginning to mount. Did that mean that there was oil under her land after all? But just as quickly she saw them vanish when she remembered that without the original drilling reports, and lacking the money to have another set of costly reports drawn up, she would never know.

A ragged little sigh escaped Catherine's lips as she folded the letter, put it back into the aged envelope, and tucked in away in the pocket of the old woolen vest. She folded the garment carefully, ran a loving hand over it, and was about to put it back when she saw the manila envelope at the bottom of the carton. What was this, more disappointment? she wondered as she opened the envelope and slid out the contents.

At first Catherine wasn't sure just what she was looking at. There were several pages of graphs and charts of dissecting lines which caused her to screw up her brows with puzzlement. It took several moments for her to realize what she held in her hands. And then she gasped. It was the long-lost drilling reports.

There were several pages of technical descriptions of the land, which made no sense to her. She learned that things like capital expenses, which included the wellhead, the pump, the pipe, and other tangibles could be depreciated over a ten-year term. And that the intangibles covered everything from the rental of the drilling rig, to special mud to lubricate the drill bits, diesel fuel to operate the rig, and labor costs. But it still didn't tell her what she needed to know.

She scrutinized the charts from every angle, searching for a hint of what they were all about, but reading them was like trying to decipher hieroglyphics. Several pages of the report appeared to be missing, frustrating her attempts even further. What did it all mean? Was there oil or wasn't there?

With trembling hands, Catherine slipped the papers back into the manila envelope. A small voice of reason in the back of her mind told her not to get her hopes up, while another voice screamed excitedly that this was her only chance to save the ranch.

There was only one thing to do. Putting practicality before pride, she tucked the envelope under her arm and left the shearing shed.

Cal was working in the east corral when she drove up. He glanced up at the peal of rapidly approaching tires, his movements grinding to a halt when he recognized the Coleman pickup. He ran the sleeve of his red plaid shirt across his brow to wipe the sweat from his eyes, turned to one of his ranch hands, and said, "Finish up for me here, would you, Ned?"

He was waiting for her by the gate when she pulled the pickup to a halt and climbed down.

"What's the matter?" he asked anxiously. "Did you find another one? Is everything okay?"

She hadn't meant to alarm him by showing up like this and sought to relieve his anxiety by answering his questions all at once. "No. Yes. I mean, everything's fine. It's this. I'd like you to look at it." Her fingers fairly shook as she slid the papers from the envelope and handed them to him.

He scanned her face, which was all flushed and anxious, looking for a clue as to the cause of her excitement before his gaze dropped to the papers she had given him. He thumbed through them in rapid succession. "This looks like . . ." He looked back up at her, confused.

"They're the drilling reports. I found them in an old carton in the shearing shed. What do you think? Can you understand what they say?" She bit her lip waiting for his response.

He was silent for several minutes as he read the information contained in the drilling reports. When he looked up at last, it was into brown eyes that were apprehensive and bright.

Her voice sank to a whisper. "Well?"

"Congratulations, Cathy," he said, his face breaking into a grin. "It's oil. And from the looks of this report, lots of it."

Excitement surged through Catherine like a hard-driven nail. Without thinking, she let out a cry of disbelief and flung her arms around his neck.

"Oh, Cal!" she cried, "Thank you, thank you, thank you!" With each expression of gratitude, she pressed a kiss to both cheeks and then to his lips.

Cal drew back, flustered by the unexpected gesture that had prompted her to kiss the scar on his left cheek. He laughed nervously and said, "Hey, Cathy, take it easy."

She grabbed the drilling reports from his hand and hugged them to her chest as she pirouetted away from him. "Do you know what this means. Oil, Cal! There's oil beneath my land!"

Amused by her happiness, he asked jokingly, "Are you giving up sheep ranching to go into the oil business?"

"Give up sheep ranching? Never! But with the proceeds from the well, I can fix up the place, hire the best shearers, buy the latest equipment, more sheep if I want."

"You're getting a little ahead of yourself, aren't you?" he pointed out.

"What do you mean?"

"What you have are drilling reports, Cathy, not a well."

"Yes, I know that. But now that I know for certain that there's oil under my land, I can hire a crew and open up that well in the northeast section."

"A crew costs money," he reminded her, and then he was sorry he had spoken when he saw the smile vanish from her beautiful face and her shoulders slump.

Money. The one thing she didn't have. In her miserable position, no bank in the world would lend her the money she needed. She thought fleetingly of her ex-husband who carried more money in his pocket than most people earned in a month, but flatly rejected the idea of going to him. She'd die first.

Catherine's gaze met Cal's in a level, straightforward look. "You offered to lend me money if I needed it."

He knew what it must have taken for her to ask. In spite of the fact that they had both discovered how they'd been duped, the doubt she had lived with all these years was slow in receding. Even when they'd made love, he had sensed that a part of her was beyond his reach. He knew also that if he had not made the offer, she would never have asked.

She would come to him for the feel of his arms around her and for the taste of his lips, and she had proved today that she would come to him for money. But would she ever come to him because she loved him?

"I'll lend you the money you need," he told her.

A breath of relief spilled from her lips. "I'll pay you back from the profits," she said. "Every penny, Cal, I promise. I'll even throw in ten cents on the dollar."

She was a clever businesswoman, but she didn't have to go that far. All she had to do was ask and he would have given her anything she wanted. Or so Cal thought, until he heard her next request.

"I'd like you to run the operation for me, Cal. You can do it, I know you can."

"No."

She was so caught up in the momentum that she didn't hear him and went on with her enthusiasm.

"I said no, Cathy."

This time there was no mistaking his refusal. She looked at him questioningly. "Why not?"

"Because . . ." He didn't know what to say.

"Because what?"

He felt himself being backed into a corner and he didn't like it. "Because I'm a cattleman, damn it, not an oil man."

"You said you did some wildcatting up north a few years ago. What's the difference?"

"Who's gonna run Pitchfork?" he argued.

"You've got ranch hands, don't you? You said yourself that you've hired the best there is."

"Damn it, Cathy," he said, his voice rising, "you don't understand."

"I'm trying to, but you aren't making any sense."

Cal pivoted on his boot heels and stalked away, leaving a bewildered Catherine standing there looking at his back.

Running to catch up with him, she grasped his arm and said, "Cal, please, what is it? What's the matter?"

He shook her off. "I said no, and that's all there is to it."

"Why are you being so pigheaded?" she demanded, her own voice losing its control. "I need your help. I can't do it without you. Do you know what it cost me to come here today and ask this? Don't you think I have pride, too?"

He stopped in his tracks and glared at her, his green eyes cutting her like glass. "Don't talk to me about pride, Cathy. Yeah, you've got pride. But I'll tell you what you don't have. You don't have *this*." He jerked his head around and pointed an accusing finger at the scar on his left cheek.

She recalled the night they had made love in his bed and she had questioned him afterwards about the scar on his face. His only comment had been a deeply-uttered vow never to go near another drilling rig again.

In a low, accusing voice she said, "You're afraid."

"You're damned right I'm afraid. You don't know what you're asking me to do."

"Then why don't you tell me?"

Cal was seized by an impulse to run. He turned away from Catherine's questions and scanned the surroundings. There was no place he could run to that would shield him from the answers. A slow and inevitable realization descended over him. The air went out of his lungs in a long, low whoosh and his shoulders slumped with resignation. He could no longer turn away from the bitter memory.

She followed him to a big cottonwood where she sat down beside him on the ground and waited for many long, tense minutes for him to speak.

The story emerged slowly at first, and then in torrents of words and emotions as Cal relived for Catherine that terrible day from the past.

It happened up in the Northwest Territories, where he'd gone to escape the pain of what he thought was her betrayal, and where the oil rig on which he was working exploded suddenly and violently.

It was all a blur after that—the days spent recuperating in the hospital with broken bones and contusions, his face swathed in bandages. He had no idea what to expect the day they took off the gauze. They were such ugly, black stitches with little knots of thread holding his flesh together. The scar was like a red-hot brand on his cheek, the pain of losing Cathy like cold steel in his heart.

The sight of his scar hadn't particularly bothered him. He'd seen a lot worse on the ranch. But a stitched-up bull was different from a stitched-up man, as Cal soon discovered.

It was afterwards that the real nightmare began. He soon learned that most women were repelled by the scar. Those who weren't were drawn to it in a lurid kind of way, as if they expected him to sling them over his shoulder and carry them off into his cave. Either way, it made not getting involved a way of life. There had been one or two women over the years who treated him as if the disfigurement didn't matter, but it hadn't worked out. He had written them off to bad timing, unable to admit to them or to himself that the feelings simply hadn't been there.

Not a day had gone by that he had not looked at his scar in the mirror while shaving, or caught a glimpse of it in a store window, or through the rear-view mirror of his pickup, and not been reminded of Cathy and the part she had played in putting the mark on him. As long as he could remember, there had been only one woman who'd meant anything to him. And she was sitting beside him now, her beautiful face dappled with sunshine, asking the impossible.

Despite the cool autumn air his shirt was soaking wet. His breath felt short in his chest. All these years he'd suppressed the memory, refusing to acknowledge it even to himself. Now that it was out, had anything changed?

Catherine's voice held none of the guilt that he had expected to hear, only a softly-uttered declaration. "We all live with fear, Cal. The trick is not to let it stop you."

He snorted derisively at that and said, "Yeah, well, whoever told you that should have his head examined. Let me guess. Angus, right?"

"Wrong. It was you who said that to me once. It was a long time ago, but it's as true for you now as it was for me then."

Cal didn't remember the occasion on which he had expounded that particular bit of wisdom, nor did he appreciate having his words thrown back at him. "I can give you the money," he told her, "but I don't know about the rest. It goes deep, Cathy, real deep."

Catherine got to her feet and brushed the dirt off her jeans. She looked down at him for some moments. Scar or no scar, he was handsome in her eyes and her heart still tripped at the sight of him.

"Cal," she said softly, "for what it's worth, I'm sorry . . . so sorry . . ." Her voice died away foolishly. As if an apology could erase the pain he must be feeling.

All those years of suppressing his feelings for her had turned Cal into a cautious man. But this was Cathy, he reminded himself, as he stared up into familiar dark eyes. Cathy in trouble and needing him. And he could no more turn her down than he'd been able to stop himself from loving her.

Cal looked into Catherine's brown eyes and saw all of her own fears expressed in them, and at that moment he forgot about his own. He knew then that he would help her. He would use his own money to buy the equipment she needed and hire the crew to get the rig going. And if she wanted him to run the damned thing for her, he'd do that, too. And maybe, just maybe one day she might love him again.

ELEVEN

As autumn leaves swirled on gusts of wind, the excitement of the drilling that was underway in the northeast section was overshadowed by an ever-growing sense of danger closer to home. The latest count of the flock revealed three more sheep missing. After several weeks without incident, Catherine was understandably rattled.

On a brisk morning in late October, she shrugged into a jacket on her way out the door, calling to Gertie, "I'll see you later."

The crisp cold air nipped at her cheeks as she strode across the lawn and headed for the barn. She thrust her hands into her pockets and walked into the wind, eyes down, mired in thought. When she rounded the corner of the barn, she looked up and halted dead in her tracks. The pickup truck was gone.

Catherine issued a loud expletive. Her plan to drive over to the drilling site was thwarted. She cast a disgusted look over at the station wagon that was still sitting beneath the trees, covered in a blanket of fallen leaves. Weeks ago she had replaced the brake fluid herself, but for some reason hadn't been able to get the darned thing started and had given it up for dead.

Where had Ben gone? she grumbled to herself. Why wasn't he here to turn out the flocks? Did she have to do everything herself?

Catherine pivoted on her boot heels and stalked off in the direction of the pen, calling for Sam. When the dog didn't appear, she looked around but couldn't find him. She could feel her blood pressure rising. The day hadn't even begun and so far nothing had gone right.

Doing an abrupt 180°, she spun around and stalked to the barn. Minutes later she emerged astride Bing. From her vantage point atop the buckskin gelding, she scanned the area, calling Sam's name and giving a familiar whistle that should have brought him running. That was odd, she thought. Sam was always with the flock. Concluding that Ben must have taken the sheepdog along with him, she turned Bing's head toward the pen, where she leaned over in the saddle to unlatch the gate.

The docile creatures baa'd as the big horse moved among them and gently herded them out the gate.

The hillsides and forests were ablaze with autumn color, and the ground was strewn with a carpet of rustling leaves. The air was crisp and cold, and overhead the sun shone in the perpetually blue Albertan sky.

Catherine guided the flock to the fenced pasture and dismounted. She wasn't certain what made her linger when there was work to be done back at the ranch. It was a feeling mostly. Nothing she could put her finger on. She tied Bing's reins to a tree, and for more than an hour, while the sheep grazed, she scoured the area, searching for clues to the mysterious disappearance of her sheep and the awful sense of foreboding that lay in the pit of her stomach.

She explored the area, poking under bushes and behind fallen logs. Eventually, her search led her down to the creek that ran the length of the pasture. There, in the soft damp earth of the bank, she found the unmistakable tracks of a wolf.

Catherine was the first to admit that wolves had taken a bad rap in recent years. There was nothing to indicate that they were the menace that farmers and ranchers claimed them to be. Nevertheless, here was possible proof to the contrary. Who knew? Perhaps the sheep that had died of the tick bite was an isolated incident. Maybe the poisoning of the ewe was just a bizarre occurrence, a tragic mistake that would never be repeated or explained. Maybe Ben was right and it was wolves all along that had been killing her sheep.

Catherine walked away from the creek feeling foolish for the way she had panicked, and guilty for having wondered if Ben were somehow responsible for what was going on. She was about to climb back into the saddle, but paused with her foot in the stirrup when something on the ground caught her eye and drew her closer for a better look.

It was a cluster of rocks that looked as if someone had painted them red. Upon closer examination, Catherine gasped when she realized that it was blood.

This was it, she thought with a small surge of triumph. This was the proof she'd been searching for that wolves were killing her sheep. And while it didn't explain how the predators had gotten past Sam, at least the discovery helped put to rest many of her troubling doubts.

But whatever sense of relief Catherine felt was painfully short-lived when she heard a muffled groan from nearby and followed it to a small clump of brush. Parting the branches, she gave out with a cry when she found Sam lying there.

The dog looked barely alive. His breathing was shallow, and there was dried blood matting his coat. Judging from the wolf tracks by the creek, Catherine's first thought was that he'd had a run-in with one of the predators. But then she spotted the broken piece of a tree limb laying in the grass. It, too, was caked with dried blood, and she didn't know what to think.

There was no time to ponder the situation. After determining that Sam was still alive, Catherine sprang into action. Among the fallen leaves she found two tree limbs that had apparently broken off in a storm. She raced back to Bing, hastily untied the reins and led him to the spot soiled with blood.

From around the saddle horn she pulled the coil of rope that Angus had taught her to always carry with her when she went riding. Most likely, he had never have anticipated the use to which she would put it now, but she was glad for the advice as she worked swiftly to fasten the broken tree limbs to Bing's saddle. Without thinking twice, she tore off her jacket and rigged it to the ends of the limbs that trailed on the ground, so that the end result was a crude but effective travois.

Sam whimpered with pain when she carefully

lifted him out from under the thicket and placed him on the travois to transport him back home. The cold air whipped about her face and chilled her to the bone, but Catherine curbed the impulse to spur Bing to go faster, careful not to cause poor Sam any more pain than he was already suffering.

Gertie came running from the house at the sound of Catherine's excited call. Together, the two women carried Sam inside where they spread a blanket before the fireplace and laid him down on it. While Gertie ran to fetch a basin of warm water and medical supplies, Catherine lit a fire to chase the chill out of the animal's bones. Then she sat down beside him and sponged the blood from his ragged coat, crooning to him as she did and praying that he would not die.

Angus had raised Sam from a pup and trained him to be one of the best sheep herding dogs around. He was a cross between a border collie and a Shetland sheepdog and possessed the best traits of each breed. It was his nature to obey willingly and naturally, with an inborn instinct to guard the flocks from invaders of all kinds. His ability to run swiftly and jump with agility over obstacles always made him a delight to watch. But what most endeared him to Catherine was his devoted, docile nature and that keen and all-but-human intelligence and understanding that made him look up at her now with those big brown eyes as if he knew she was there to help him.

Hovering overhead, Gertie questioned anxiously, "Shouldn't we get him to a vet?"

"We can't," she replied. "Ben took the truck. Where'd he go, anyway?"

"I don't know," said Gertie. "He's been gone since early this morning."

Catherine ran a loving hand over Sam's quivering coat. "Don't worry, boy, we'll take care of you." She began a slow, methodical examination, probing carefully for broken bones.

"What happened to him?" Gertie asked.

She answered simply, "Wolf."

Gertie leaned in closer and screwed up her expression. "I don't see any bites. It looks to me like he's been hit with something."

Catherine's fingers tripped in their ministrations. She was startled to hear Gertie verbalize what she herself was thinking, and shivered at the thought of the bloodied tree limb. Not wishing to alarm Gertie, however, she said, "That's ridiculous. Who would do something like that? Besides, I saw the wolf tracks with my own eyes."

Nothing appeared to be broken, so after the wound was cleansed Catherine applied the antiseptic salve that Gertie found in the medicine chest, figuring that if it was good enough for people, then it was good enough for Sam. After that, she worked carefully to wrap his midsection with the gauze strips that Gertie cut and handed to her.

It hurt Catherine to see the once vibrant animal lying helpless and inert. She went quickly to the telephone and dialed Drew Devlin's office number. The receptionist informed her in a supercilious tone, which grated instantly on Catherine's already frazzled nerves, that he was in surgery. And besides, he didn't make house calls. Catherine slammed the receiver down.

"Damn it. What else can possibly go wrong?" she

complained as she stomped upstairs. Moments later, she reappeared pulling a sweatshirt on over her head.

"Watch him closely, Gertie. I'm riding over to the well." Her voice tightened noticeably when she added, "Hopefully, by the time I get back, Ben will have returned."

Outside, Catherine muttered to herself as she dismantled the makeshift travois. Her jacket ruined from blood and grass stains, she gave it an irritable toss aside and mounted Bing with graceful determination. With a jerk of the reins, she turned his head northeast and galloped off.

In the last few weeks, Catherine had driven to the well site on several occasions to check on the progress of the drilling. She didn't allow herself to dwell on the possibilities, having learned the hard way that dreams do not always come true. Still, she could not help but be guilty of an occasional *what if?*

True to Cal's word, he worked tirelessly, dividing his time between running Pitchfork and supervising the drilling of Catherine's well. On this particular day she found him down on one knee, bent over the papers that were spread on the ground before him. His dark hair curled over the collar of his jacket that was turned up against the autumnal nip. Occasionally, he would reach up to absently swipe at an errant lock blown into his eyes by the wind.

The deep-throated growl of heavy engines and pumping machinery made it necessary for Catherine to shout to be heard over the din.

"Anything?" she asked as she approached. Her pulse quickened when those beautiful green eyes looked up and focused on her.

"Not yet. It could be days, it could be weeks."

Inwardly, she groaned. She couldn't afford to wait weeks.

Cal rolled up the papers and handed the cylinders to the man who'd been studying them with him. Both men stood up and spoke a few more words together before the other walked off. When Cal turned back to Catherine, he dropped all pretense of cordiality by demanding, "What's wrong?"

She knew it was useless to evade him. He would only hound it out of her. "It's Sam," she said. "He's been hurt bad. He may have had a run-in with a wolf." But even as she said it she didn't really believe it.

His deep voice rose above the noise, sounding faintly suspicious. "Have wolves ever bothered your sheep before?"

"Not that I know of. I guess Sam did a good job of keeping them away until now."

"Wolves don't usually bother the stock when there's a dog on guard."

Catherine shrugged as if to suggest that her guess was as good as his. "Sam's getting old. Maybe the wolves sensed it and took advantage of it."

He replied skeptically, "I've only known wolves to attack the stock in the winter, when there's not enough game around and they're starving. But there's plenty of prey out there for them." He looked at her closely, sensing that there was more to it than she was saying. "Is there something you're not telling me, Cathy?" A look of alarm sped across his handsome face. "Have you lost any more sheep?"

She looked away nervously. All around her men were working like bees in a hive, sinking the drill bit deeper into the ground in search of the valuable crude. One of the men waved to her from across the distance. Numbly, Catherine waved back.

She couldn't bring herself to tell Cal about the sheep, not after he'd done so much for her already by putting aside his own legitimate fears to get the rig going. No, she decided, she wouldn't burden him with any more of her problems.

"Of course not. I'm just feeling paranoid, that's all." She laughed, but it was a strained sound that scratched at the back of her throat.

She could be so damned stubborn at times that he didn't press the issue. Still, he wasn't the kind of man to keep his opinions to himself.

"I don't like the idea of you being alone in that house," he griped.

"I'm not alone," she insisted. "I've got Ben and Gertie with me."

"That's not what I mean and you know it." His tone softened a little. "Why don't you come out to Pitchfork and stay for a while? Take a break from it all."

She looked at him with a horrified expression. "I can't do that! There's too much work to do. And now, without Sam, it's going to be even tougher."

Cal's whole body stiffened. "Is that all it is, Cathy?"

"What do you mean?"

"I mean that maybe there's another reason why you don't want to stay at Pitchfork."

"What other reason could there possibly be?"

Did she think he couldn't see through her facade? He was seized by an impulse to grip her by the shoulders and shake some sense into her. Instead, he clamped a firm hand over her arm and pulled her non too gently aside and out of earshot of the men who worked all around them.

"You're afraid," he said, his tone low and accusing. "Don't deny it. I can see it in your eyes. Don't you think I am, too? Christ, Cathy, I went through my own private hell for ten years."

She looked into his scorching green eyes and felt his fingers trembling about her arm, and she grew a little afraid.

Cal muttered a curt epithet and released her. Why was she resisting his efforts to close the gap between them, making him feel like a damned fool for his effort?

"Forget it, Cathy. It won't work. I tried to tell myself it might. That maybe just having you underneath me like I'd imagined it a million times in my mind would be enough. But it's not. It can never be enough. With you and me, it's gotta be all or nothing at all."

She saw the disappointment in his eyes as he spoke, and heard the sharp edge of bitterness in his voice, and felt a stab of agony like a dagger through her heart. She didn't want to hurt him, not after everything he'd done for her. She wanted to believe him, to trust him, to put all her faith in him—not just for the drilling of the well, but for a lifetime. But she was afraid to.

"You don't understand!" she cried. "I'm on the brink of losing the ranch, my livelihood. How can I take the chance of getting involved with you all over again and risk losing it all?" Her eyes pleaded with him for understanding, but the hard, implacable look she saw stamped on his face told her it would not be forthcoming.

Catherine could feel the panic rising within. Why had she come here today? What had she hoped to gain? The fact was, in the wake of Sam's injury she hadn't thought, she had simply acted. Swept up in fear and confusion, she had turned to the one person in the world who might offer some solace. What she got instead was an ultimatum.

Her voice emerged as a choked whisper. "I lost you once and it nearly destroyed me. If it ever happened again . . ." She could not verbalize the dreaded possibility.

Unable to keep the urgency out of the question, he asked, "What could happen that hasn't already happened? We were fools, Cathy. Kids who didn't know any better. We believed the lies. But we don't have to believe them anymore."

She closed her eyes in agony. "I don't know what to believe any more."

"Believe this," he growled.

Without warning he reached for her again. She was in his arms before her eyes had snapped fully open. He crushed her mouth beneath his, making her wince at the scrape of his teeth across her lip. He didn't care who was watching or who didn't like it. He had a point to make. And when he released her and stepped back, his own chest heaving mightily from the rush of blood through his veins, he saw the heated blush on her cheeks, the lusty fires in her eyes, and heard the quickness of her breath, and he knew that his point had been well taken.

She could deny everything else, but let her deny *that*, Cal thought as he turned on his boot heels and stalked off.

Catherine rode home feeling confused and angry.

Damn his arrogance. Who was he to deliver ultimatums? She had agreed to repay him out of the proceeds of the well, and was even going to throw in a tidy profit to the bargain. But that was all she had agreed to. She hadn't bargained for anything else, not now, not when there was so much else over which she was uncertain.

She had called it paranoia, but it was more than that. If she didn't know better, she could swear that someone was intent upon driving her out of business. But for the life of her, she didn't know why . . . or who.

By the time Catherine got home, a terrible fear had engulfed her. It was the fear of being alone, of not having a strong shoulder to lean against, nor strong arms to wind around her, nor a soft voice to tell her that everything would be all right. She had a sudden, intense longing for Cal, for the feel of his warm, wet mouth, the pressure of his strong, male body along the length of hers. Upstairs in her bedroom she flung herself down on the bed and wept into the pillow. *Oh, Cal,* she cried softly, *how I need you.*

If only she were able to put aside these desperate fears and give him what he wanted, and what she wanted, too. Here she was, needing him, longing for the safe haven of his arms to take her away from all this self-doubt and the danger that lurked within and without; yet knowing all along that it was her own fear of loving him again that was keeping them apart and making her miserable.

Her tears had dried by the time she heard the sound of tires pulling into the gravel driveway. She sprang from the bed and went to the window. Ben had returned.

In the bathroom Catherine washed her face and combed her hair. Then she put on her bravest face and went downstairs.

Ben was just coming through the door when she appeared at the foot of the stairs.

"I hope your errand was important," she said icily. "I'd hate to think that we might lose Sam because I couldn't get him to the vet in time."

It was then he saw the dog lying before the hearth. "What happened?"

"That's what I'm about to find out. Can I have the keys to the truck?"

Ben remained tight lipped as he helped Catherine carry Sam outside and place him in the rear of the pickup. Catherine climbed into the cab and started up the engine. Rolling down the window, she said to him, "You'll have to use Bing to get the flocks in."

Stiffly, he asked, "Where are you taking him?"

"To Edmonton."

He knew that she meant to Devlin, and was about to protest.

"No arguments, Ben," she said, cutting him off. "I'm tired, and there's been enough damage done for one day."

Catherine didn't think things could get any worse, but she found out otherwise when she arrived in Edmonton. Drew Devlin wasn't in the office. According to his receptionist, he was at the university.

"You told me earlier that he was in surgery," Catherine protested.

The woman responded defensively. "Look, Miss Coleman, I'm just following instructions. If he tells me to tell people that he's in surgery, then he's in surgery. If he says he going to the university, then he's going to the university. I only work here."

Catherine reined in her mounting frustration before it could explode into fury. There was no sense in taking her problems out on innocent bystanders.

"You're right. I'm sorry. It's not your fault. It's been a bad day. My dog's been hurt bad and I need to get him to a vet. I know you work for Doctor Devlin, and I wouldn't ask this if it weren't an emergency, but do you think you can refer me to another vet close by? I drove all the way here, and I can't drive back without having someone look at Sam. Please. I'd be so grateful."

The woman hedged with uncertainty for a moment or two as to whether or not she should oblige. This was a highly unusual request. What would Doctor Devlin think if she referred one of his clients to a competitor? In the end, it was the desperate look on Catherine's face and the imploring tone of her voice that made her relent.

"You can try the animal hospital on Jasper. But don't tell Doctor Devlin that I told you," she called out to Catherine's rapidly retreating back.

The people at the animal hospital were understanding of the emergency and admitted Sam posthaste. Catherine said good-bye to her beloved pet and left him in their safekeeping.

Dusk was descending over the foothills by the time she turned onto the narrow dirt road that led toward home. Little did she know that the day which had started out on a bad note was about to come crashing to an end.

TWELVE

Ben McFarland drove northwest along Highway 43, past fertile farmlands, past Whitecourt where the Mcleod and Eagle Rivers met with Beaver Creek; past untamed forested wilderness that abounded with big game like moose, elk, deer, and bear; past lakes that teemed with northern pike, whitefish, and perch; past the oil fields that made this area a thriving center. At the junction of Highways 43 and 34, surrounded by fields of wheat, oats, barley, and canola, he turned off onto the road that would take him home, although just how long it would remain his home was anybody's guess.

It seemed to Ben as if he'd been driving all day, first to Leduc, then to Red Deer. He was tired and irritable, and worried, most of all worried. This was one day he wished had never happened.

Earlier in the day Ben had returned from his trip to Leduc bearing grim news. He hadn't told Catherine about the dead sheep he'd found several days ago, nor that in spite of her preference for Drew Devlin, he'd taken the carcass to the vet in Leduc. He had felt even less inclined to tell her this morning that he was driving back to Leduc for a consultation with the vet over the autopsy results. Having risked Catherine's ire, and most likely his job, by taking the carcass to Leduc, he had planned on owning up to it and facing the consequences. But that was before he found out that the animal had been poisoned. It was only when he'd returned home and heard about Sam that he realized his error in keeping his mission a secret.

He felt miserable about Sam, of course, but how was he to know that the dog would need medical attention while he'd taken the truck to Leduc?

Things had happened fast after that. Catherine had driven off to Edmonton with Sam, her abrupt departure having left Ben feeling frustrated and helpless. To make matters worse, Gertie had been upset and had begun to cry. Ben had figured that the best thing to do was get his wife over to her folks in Red Deer until this mess blew over. Besides, if he was going to be fired, at least Gertie didn't have to be there to witness it. He had his pride, after all.

But Catherine had taken the pickup truck to Edmonton, leaving only the incapacitated station wagon. Ben had cursed his luck at being without a vehicle. There had been only one thing to do. With a wrench in hand and a look of angry determination fixed on his face, he had stalked outside to fix the damned thing. What he found shocked him.

The slice in the brake line was evident when he crawled beneath the car to survey the damage. So *that's* what Catherine had been alluding to each time the subject had come up. Good Lord, did she think it was his fault? He had wondered angrily why she hadn't just come right out and asked him. No doubt, that stubborn Scottish pride of hers had prevented her from doing so.

In a way, though, he admired her for it. If it weren't for that relentless pride of hers, she would have thrown in the towel on the ranch long ago, as most others would have. But not her. She was a fighter, a survivor. She had guts, that one did. Sure, she was proud to a fault, and arrogant enough to drive a man crazy. And he had to admit he hadn't liked it one bit when she showed up and began running things. But Ben's feelings of resentment had always been tempered by a grudging respect for Catherine's courage. And then, of course, there was Gertie always nagging at him, telling him to give Catherine her due, that the woman had more spunk and valor than ten men combined. In retrospect, Ben was obliged to admit that it was true.

In the barn he'd found a can of brake fluid that Catherine had purchased in her vain attempt to replace what the car had lost. In less than an hour he had repaired the damage, hustled Gertie into the car, and sped off in the direction of Red Deer.

There was no doubt in Ben's mind that someone had cut the brake line of Catherine's car. But who? And why? Then Ben recalled that it had happened the day she'd taken that carcass into Edmonton, and that started him to thinking.

He'd never cared for the likes of Drew Devlin. It was nothing specific, just things he'd heard here and there that gave him the impression that the man cared more for money than for animals. His uneasy suspicions of Devlin's veterinary ability were compounded by the autopsy report and by the opinion of the vet in Leduc that it wasn't likely that a tick bite would kill a healthy sheep.

Sheep tick, my eye, Ben grumbled to himself as his fingers tightened around the steering wheel. *Viral infection? Fat chance!* He no longer even thought that wolves were to blame for the loss in livestock. If a wolf had killed the sheep, then it was the two-legged variety.

Yet, even with the disturbing report he'd received earlier, Ben had no reason to suspect Drew Devlin guilty of anything more than superfluous veterinary procedures. All that shiny new equipment and those framed diplomas didn't make the man a good veterinarian, not by a long shot. Nor had there been any reason to think that the expensive clothes and flashy car were indicative of anything more than a greedy nature. No reason at all to suspect where such greed would lead.

Now, alone with his thoughts on the lonely stretch of highway that led home, a crazy notion began to form in his mind. At first it seemed too farfetched to be possible. But was it?

There were just too many things that didn't make sense. With so many loose ends, Ben could come up with only one common denominator . . . Drew Devlin.

If what Ben suspected was true, he knew that Catherine was going to need all the help she could get. He knew also that there was only one person who could help her, and that was Cal Walker. He'd made no secret of his dislike for Cal, but, hell, now wasn't the time for personal feelings to get in the way of what he had to do.

Armed only with his suspicions and a deep, abiding feeling in his gut that he had stumbled onto something, he decided that the first thing he would do when he got home was call Cal.

The phone was ringing when he walked in the front door. He rushed to it and mumbled a gruff hello into the receiver.

"What? Oh my God. Yes, yes, I'll tell her."

Ben dropped the receiver back into the cradle and glared down at the telephone, hating it for the news it had just delivered, hating even more the task that had fallen into his lap—the task of relaying that news to Catherine.

He didn't have long to wait. Moments later he heard the sound of tires on the gravel driveway.

Catherine knew something was wrong the instant she walked in the door and saw the ashen look on Ben's face. Her heart leaped into her throat.

"What is it?" she asked, her voice rising. "Where's Gertie?"

"I drove her to Red Deer."

"Red Deer? Why?"

He hardly knew where to begin. There was so much to tell. "Catherine, there's been an explosion at the well."

Everything went cold inside of her. She moved her lips as if to speak, but only one word emerged. "Cal . . ."

Ben swallowed hard and said, "They took him to the hospital about an hour ago. Catherine, wait! There's something else you should know!"

But it was too late to stop her. She was already out the door.

Ben watched her red tail lights disappear into the growing twilight and walked with heavy steps back inside. Without thinking, but somehow knowing exactly what he was doing, he went to the phone and dialed the number of the hospital.

Cal had been lying there in the hospital bed as if in a trance, desperately trying to regroup his senses, asking himself over and over again what the odds were of an explosion like that ever happening a second time, and hoping that it was all nothing more than a bad dream from which he would eventually awaken, when the phone rang beside the bed.

He wondered what the hell Ben McFarland was up to by asking if he could come by the hospital.

"I'm in no mood for riddles, McFarland," Cal said irritably. "If you have something to say, say it."

"It's Catherine," Ben grumbled on the other end of the line. "I think she's in trouble."

In those few seconds Cal weighed the urgency he heard in Ben's voice against everything he knew about him which, admittedly, wasn't very much. His instincts told him to put his preconceived ideas about Ben McFarland aside—to at least listen to the man.

"What kind of trouble?" he demanded.

Ben went as silent as a rock. Then, "I can't discuss it over the phone."

Cal issued an expletive under his breath. "There's a diner on Jasper. The Blue Bay. You know it?"

"Yeah, sure."

"Meet me there." He hung up without giving the other man a chance to respond.

Neither the doctor's protest nor Cal's own weakened condition could prevent him from getting up from that hospital bed and checking himself out. It was a lucky thing that the men at the well had used his own pickup truck to transport him to the hospital after the explosion. He found the vehicle sitting beneath a street lamp in the parking lot. He had difficulty getting the key into the ignition because of a badly burned and bandaged right hand, and he groaned in agony when he attempted to shift. But the pain was secondary next to the sense of urgency he felt building up inside of him.

The look in Ben's eyes when he walked in the door made Cal's guard go up immediately. Ben slid into the seat opposite Cal in the booth.

"All right, McFarland, what's so damned important?"

Cal listened in tight-lipped silence, green eyes fixed hard on Ben's face as Ben told him about the autopsy report of the vet in Leduc. His fists clenched in wordless fury atop the formica table, the burns on his right hand no longer even noticeable.

"Damn," he seethed through clenched teeth. "She brought a carcass over to me, too. My vet's report also indicated poison."

Surprise registered on Ben's face. "Did she know that?"

"Of course, she did. I told her. Did you tell her what you found out?"

Ben looked away guiltily and shook his head. "She would've been mad as a hornet if she'd known I'd taken that carcass to Leduc." He looked back at Cal and said defensively, "That doesn't excuse me for not telling her, mind you. And I was going to. But when she heard about the explosion at the well, she lit out of there like her tail was on fire."

Cal shook his head with angry understanding. "Yeah, that sounds like Cathy."

"There's more," said Ben. He ran his tongue over his lips in a nervous motion, drew in a deep breath, and told Cal about the severed brake line.

"Cut?" Cal leaned menacingly across the formica table, eyes burning into Ben's like hard green stones. "What do you mean, cut?"

"Cut, I'm telling you. With a knife."

Cal could feel his fury bubbling, threatening to explode. He waved away the waitress who appeared at the table to take their orders, and said, "Do you have any idea who would do something like that?"

Ben swallowed and said, "Drew Devlin."

"What proof do you have?"

"None."

"Then what makes you think he'd do something like that?"

"I don't know. It's just a feeling I have somewhere in here." Ben pointed to his gut. "I can't seem to shake it."

Cal ran a weary hand through his dark hair, sweeping the rumpled locks from his forehead. He was oblivious to the relentless throbbing of the bruise at his forehead, which had rendered him unconscious not so very long ago. For a man who had always trusted his own instincts, he wasn't so quick to dispel Ben's, no matter how farfetched they sounded.

"I never liked that guy," Ben was saying. "There's something about him."

"That's funny," said Cal. "Cathy said the same thing about him. It never made any difference to me because I have my own vet at Pitchfork. He's supposed to be good, though. That's why she went to him in the first place. She was desperate, man. I could see it. She was losing her sheep and didn't know what to do. Hell, I would have done the same thing." He leveled a hard look at Ben, as if daring him to fault Catherine for the decision she'd made, no matter how wrong it may have been.

"Good?" Ben echoed. "I don't know how good the guy is. Tell me something, Walker. Have you heard of any unusual outbreaks of sheep tick this season?"

"No, I haven't."

"Neither have I. But that's what Devlin said killed the sheep Catherine took to him for autopsy. Now, I'm not saying it wasn't sheep tick, but I'm also not saying it was. And I'm not saying that Devlin's responsible for anything, but you gottà admit, it looks downright suspicious. The accident happened the day she drove to Edmonton to see him. The conflicting autopsy reports. Something pretty damned fishy is going on here."

"You're right," said Cal. "Where's Cathy?"

"She drove off to the hospital as soon as she heard about the explosion."

Cal realized suddenly where his impulsive actions had led. He wished now that he had met with Ben at the hospital, instead of pig-headedly insisting on this place whose bright fluorescent lights only made his head hurt more. He should have known that Catherine would be at the hospital, resistant, doubtful, and trying hard not to show her fears, but there. If he had stayed, he could have warned her of the danger she was in.

Cal had no idea if Ben's hunches were correct. But the growing sickness in the pit of his belly told him one thing for certain. Catherine was in terrible trouble.

THIRTEEN

Catherine pleaded and begged, yelled and threatened, and even let loose with a string of salty invectives, but the battered old pickup truck just wouldn't go any faster. The speedometer hovered around fifty-five, and the engine made a straining sound.

"Oh, please," she begged, "don't break down."

She had to get to the hospital before it was too late. After all the excuses she had given herself and all the obstacles she had placed in her path, in spite of all the fears and doubts, she had to get there in time to tell him how much she loved him. How much she had always loved him.

She drove with her eyes focused on the road ahead, but her mind was light years away. Whoever would have thought when she'd returned to this place after ten years of voluntary exile that she would be speeding at this moment like a madwoman to . . . To what? With a flash of desperation she realized that she wasn't really sure. To Cal, of course, to tell him what she should have told him long before this, but beyond that Catherine dared not speculate.

All or nothing at all, isn't that what he'd told her? All right then, even if he didn't love her the way she loved him, she would be the one to break the ten-year silence during which time not a single word of love had been uttered between them.

Every time she contemplated the risks of getting involved with Cal all over again, she would think of the past. Each time she considered happiness, she would remember how easily her dreams of happiness had been shattered. She could not deny that she was afraid . . . terrified was more like it. But neither could she deny the presence in her soul of the man who had been her first and only love. She had never really succeeded in casting him out of her heart, and it had taken that first fleeting glimpse of him through the shadows in a rain-soaked shack for her to know it. How utterly stupid she had been to think she could live without him. What a fool to have even tried.

"Faster," she urged the pickup. "Faster!"

Catherine's foot pressed harder on the accelerator. The truck made a valiant attempt to comply, but could not summon more speed. The engine coughed and sputtered, and Catherine did her best to control the panic that was rising within.

"Don't stop!" she cried. "Oh, please don't stop!"

After what seemed like a lifetime, she reached the hospital. She shut off the engine, and for the next few moments she just sat there as a solid wall of silence closed around her, shutting out the hubbub of the public parking lot, leaving her feeling alone and helpless with her excruciating thoughts. For the first time since she had raced out of the house, Ben's words came flooding back to her.

Explosion at the well. The words echoed off the walls of Catherine's mind like a gunshot. The color drained from her face and her legs felt weak and rubbery, scarcely capable of carrying her inside.

The silence that filled her was as awful as the cruel reality that worked its way slowly, insidiously into her thoughts. Explosion. Her body shuddered with fear. A tight, constricting feeling overwhelmed her heart, as if someone had reached a hand deep down inside and squeezed without mercy, tighter and tighter until she could no longer breathe. For all she knew, she'd arrived too late.

Catherine had no idea how long she sat there, although in reality it was only seconds. The shrill blast of a car horn in the parking lot jolted her back to reality. And then she was out of the truck and running as fast as she could, not knowing what she would find. She had no clear recollection of how she got from the parking lot to the desk, but suddenly there she was. Out of breath from running, she managed between pants to question the nurse on duty, then steeled herself for the reply.

Catherine blinked with incomprehension. "Checked out? Wh–what do you mean?"

She listened numbly as the nurse explained that Cal had been admitted earlier for treatment of some nasty burns on his right hand. There was a mild concussion, too, which had warranted overnight watching. Nevertheless, against the doctor's orders, he had checked himself out. Overwhelmed with relief to learn that Cal was all right, yet puzzled by his actions, Catherine left the hospital.

It was dark by the time she got home. When she pulled into the driveway and got out of the truck, she noticed that there were no lights on inside the house, but she was too wrapped up in her thoughts to suspect that anything was amiss. It wasn't until she climbed the creaking porch steps and saw the note tacked to the front door that she felt the first faint stirrings that something was wrong.

Unable to read the note in the darkness, she turned on the porch light. A warm yellow glow bathed her face as she scanned the words which read, "Catherine, meet me at my place." It was signed simply, "Cal."

The hairs at the back of Catherine's neck stood on end. She hesitated, unable to pinpoint the cause of it. The handwriting didn't look like Cal's, but that was understandable considering that the bandages most likely hindered his writing. Still, something about the note didn't feel quite right.

She opened the front door, thrust her head inside and called out for Ben: no answer came from anywhere in the darkened house. There was no time to wonder where he had gone. Sensing the urgency of Cal's message, Catherine rushed back outside, jumped into the truck, and drove to Pitchfork.

She wasn't surprised to see no one about as she drove up the winding driveway to the big house. The Canadian Finals Rodeo, which was currently underway in Edmonton, always drew big crowds, and no doubt Cal had given the rough and tumble Pitchfork ranch hands time off to participate in the competition and the partying that invariably followed.

Catherine was surprised, however, when Millie didn't answer her knock on the door, until she remembered that the day Cal had invited her to stay for lunch he'd mentioned something about Millie having a son-in-law who competed in rodeo events. She'd been so nervous that afternoon, having been taken by him with a force that thrilled her, struggling through lunch in anticipation of it happening again, that she'd scarcely heard a word he said; just small talk about nothing in particular, and something about Millie's son-in-law.

Well, that would account for the absence of the housekeeper, but where was Cal? She knocked again, but still there was no answer. She found it odd, particularly since the lights were on, suggesting that someone was home.

Her fingers tested the doorknob and found it unlocked. Hesitantly, she pushed the door open, poked her head in and called Cal's name. Greeted by silence, she stepped inside and closed the door softly behind her. Her footsteps moved quickly across the carpeted floorboards as she went first to the kitchen, and not finding him there, then to the staircase. Thinking that he might be upstairs taking a shower, she started confidently up the stairs.

But Cal's bedroom was dark, and there was no sound of running water coming from the adjoining bathroom.

Assuming that she had probably arrived ahead of him, Catherine was about to head back downstairs to wait for him in the parlor, when a curious impulse turned her steps in the opposite direction.

Upstairs on the third floor everything looked exactly as Catherine remembered it. Nothing had changed. Not a single piece of furniture had been moved or disturbed in all these years. The white cloths that covered the furnishings were filled with dust and yellowed with age, giving the unlived-in rooms the ghostly feel she remembered so well.

This was where she and Cal used to play hide and seek as kids. She would scramble beneath one of the shrouds and wait until he found her, and he always did, like a bee zeroing in on honey. Doing an effective imitation of Frankenstein's monster, he would chase her through the adjoining doors of the dusty rooms while she screamed, partly with terror, but mostly with delight.

Back then, the lifelessness of the rooms was overpowered by their youthful exuberance. Tonight, however, there were no sounds of laughter echoing through these lonely halls, and for the first time Catherine felt the weight of the loneliness, accompanied by an inexplicable urge to flee. Yet she did not, for this was where she had spent some of the happiest hours of her life. The memories imparted by these deserted rooms overrode the disquieting feelings. Despite the inner warnings, she lingered.

The sound of the front door closing was a faint echo when it reached Catherine's ears on the third floor. From where she stood at the fireplace in the big bedroom, gazing up at a large oil painting of the mountains that she'd always loved, she smiled and called out over her shoulder, "I'm up here, Cal!"

She was about to turn and leave the room, when she heard his footsteps coming up the stairs. She noticed no urgency to his gait, only the sure and steady thump of his boots on the hardwood floor. Since he appeared to be in no hurry, she decided not to meet him halfway, but rather to wait for him here, giving in to the impulse to see him once again among these surroundings and, for a moment or two perhaps, make the past become real. She turned back to admire the painting, confident that he would find her.

It took only moments for his steps to reach the bedroom and stop in the doorway. Catherine's heart soared as she spun around to greet him, then slammed hard against the wall of her chest when the face that looked back at her was not Cal's.

"I knocked," he said. "No one answered."

Something tensed inside of Catherine. Hadn't she heard that once before?

"Isn't anyone here?" he inquired.

"Everyone's at the rodeo in Edmonton."

"Not everyone. You're not. What brings you to Pitchfork at this hour?"

"I might ask you that same question."

"Business," he said.

She looked at him curiously. "At this hour?"

"My business isn't with Cal Walker. It's with you, Catherine."

There was something about the way he spoke her name that made her go all quiet inside. Her mind worked furiously to identify the feeling that pricked at her like hundreds of little pins. A tremble passed over her smooth flesh for a reason she did not know, and the hairs that suddenly sprang to attention at the back of her neck put her distinctly on guard.

Despite the disruptive sensation that scratched at the back of her mind, struggling to get out, Catherine said levelly, "Whatever your business is with me, it can wait. Some things are more important."

Drew Devlin had anticipated the flames that leapt into those angry brown eyes, and took her indignation in stride. "I'm not here to discuss your sheep."

Catherine remained firm in spite of the unexpected

curve. With a distinctly uncordial note in her voice, she said, "If you're not here to discuss my sheep, then I can't imagine that you and I have anything to discuss at all."

"Oh, but I assure you we do."

She bristled at the disdainful correction. "In that case, a phone call in the morning would have sufficed."

"Perhaps," Devlin offered. "But you're right, you know. Some things *are* more important than sheep. And some things just can't wait."

He moved with deceptive ease into the room and came to stand beside her before the fireplace. "Nice," he said of the oil painting she'd been admiring earlier, "but common, don't you think?"

Slowly, Catherine replied, "A matter of taste, I suppose. Personally, I prefer simple things."

"Why settle for mountains by some unknown when you can have a Renoir or a Matisse, or even a Van Gogh? All it takes is money."

"I appear to have underestimated your ambition," she said. "But tell me something. How does a veterinarian afford something as priceless as a Van Gogh?"

"By careful planning, my dear Catherine. By investing properly. By recognizing opportunity and taking advantage of it. But need you ask? You were married to such ingenuity, weren't you?"

The unexpected and unwelcome mention of Catherine's former husband made her blanch. "Yes. And if you'll notice, I'm no longer married to it. That, too, by preference."

"More's the pity," he remarked. "You could certainly use some of that ingenuity right now, couldn't you?"

"If you're referring to my ex-husband's wealth, that's no loss to me."

"Isn't it? With your well out of commission and your ranch on the brink of bankruptcy? Of course, those drilling reports must give you some idea of where to drill next time. You do have the drilling reports, don't you?" He knew she did. In her dire financial straits she would have been crazy to get that old well going again unless she'd found the original reports and knew exactly where the oil was.

Catherine put an abrupt halt to his speculation, however, by announcing, "There isn't going to be a next time."

"Giving up, are you? Hmm, that's too bad. Well, it's for the best, I suppose. Although, I feel I must level with you, Catherine. I've seen a lot of ranches go out of business with a heck of a lot more than you have."

Inwardly, Catherine groaned. Was he going to start on that subject again? "I don't see what that has to do with anything, or, for that matter, what interest you have in my affairs. Besides, Cal is due back any minute, so if you don't mind . . ."

"Ah, yes, the industrious Mister Walker. He certainly has turned this place into a money-making operation. You have to admire that. Still, it's strictly small time."

Catherine could feel the blood rushing to her face. "I'll have you know that Cal has worked harder than anyone I know to make a success of his business. The next time you sit down to a steak dinner, remember that it's probably Pitchfork beef you're eating."

It was on the tip of her tongue to tell him that Cal Walker was a hundred times more of a man than the mealy-mouthed, white-skinned excuse for one who stood before her talking about wealth and Van Goghs as if those things could give him something he would never have . . . class.

''Didn't there used to be something between you two?'' he asked. ''Oh,'' he exclaimed, as if a thought had just occurred to him. ''Perhaps there still is.'' He could tell by the sudden flush of her cheeks that he was right on target, but he'd expected as much. ''Well then, let's hope he's all right.''

Cautiously, Catherine responded. ''Why wouldn't he be?''

''Those well explosions can be nasty business.''

''How did you know about the explosion?''

''News of that kind travels fast. Like the news that you're about to go under. Although that's hardly news, is it? You know, Catherine, you really should consider selling that place. As a matter of fact, that's what I want to discuss with you.''

She couldn't believe his infernal persistence. ''Let me guess. You want to buy it.''

''I'd be willing to take it off your hands,'' he conceded.

''What on earth for?'' His response to her facetious remark shocked her.

''Let's just say for old times' sake.'' In answer to the look of utter incredulity on her face, he added, ''My uncle and your grandfather were such good friends, it's the least I can do.''

''I would hardly call a near-bankrupt sheep ranch a wise investment,'' she pointed out.

''True. But with my money I could possibly make

something of it. Your only alternative is to watch it go under.''

She couldn't deny the awful truth of what he was saying. She had hoped to use the proceeds from the well to get the ranch back on its feet and to keep Angus's dream alive. To watch it crumble around her was as painful as anything else she had ever experienced. But as surely as Catherine knew that, she knew also that her grandfather's Scot's pride would have seen the place die before selling out to a man like Drew Devlin.

Her chin tilted up at him in that way he'd come by now to recognize as her impossible stubbornness. ''I'm sorry. It's not for sale.''

''That's regrettable. It truly is.''

Catherine detested the feigned concern. ''It's my problem. I'll deal with it.''

He expelled a sigh of impatience and shook his head. ''Unfortunately, Catherine, it has also become my problem.''

There is was again, that queasiness that came whenever he spoke her name. Something about it sent warning bells off in her mind. *What could it be?* she wondered frantically.

It came to Catherine slowly, not like a bolt from out of the blue, but in gradual degrees of realization, each one more acute and terrible than the one preceding it, until she knew with sudden clarity what it was that had put her on edge from the beginning of this strained conversation.

The note tacked to her front door had not been addressed to Cathy, as Cal always called her, but to Catherine, as this man called her.

Catherine looked back at him with new understanding and a sickness welling in the pit of her stomach. "How did you know I was here?"

An unwelcome line stretched across Drew Devlin's mouth, a semblance of a smile as he looked back at her with cold, unfeeling eyes. She knew about the note. He could see it on her face. Damn the clever little bitch for having figured it out. Well, that settled it. If there'd been any doubt in his mind before as to what he must do, it was gone now. The little fool had sealed her own fate.

Devlin's expression remained level, although inwardly he paled. "So, it appears there is no need for us to pretend any longer, is there?"

He sauntered to the white-shrouded sofa that stood before the fireplace, pulled off the cloth and sat down. Patting the seat beside him, he said, "Come, Catherine, have a seat, and I'll explain everything."

She remained rooted to her spot, her dark eyes hostile and untrusting.

He shrugged with a careless lifting of his shoulders. "As you wish."

He began with a sigh, speaking in a voice that was surprisingly soft, a sign that should have warned Catherine to flee.

"I learned years ago from my uncle about the oil beneath Angus's land. To be frank, I had forgotten all about it until only a few months ago when I was going through some of my uncle's things and I found a cancelled check made out to your grandfather. You know, I had often wondered where that old man got the money to drill for oil. I never guessed that my uncle had given it to him. My uncle, you see, had the disastrous habit of thinking with his heart instead of his brain. Be that as it may, that's what started me thinking. Oil. How interesting. What possibilities." He chuckled in a self-satisfied manner. "That's when I began to plan."

He settled back into the sofa and folded his hands comfortably across his chest, quite as if he was enjoying torturing her with every little revelation. "I thought at first that if I got rid of some of your sheep, that foreman of yours would either resign or be fired, and that would speed up the demise of the place."

The fulsome smile soured behind a dangerous glint in his eyes. "I was well on my way toward that end when you showed up at the beginning of the summer. I tried to scare you off by poisoning a few of your sheep and disposing of the carcasses."

Catherine felt sick inside. So, there had been no virus after all, no need for her and Ben to work so hard to vaccinate the flocks. No antibiotic in the world would have protected them against the poison he'd been administering. There had been no attacks by wolves either, no outbreaks of sheep tick, nothing destroying her flocks except the deviousness of this one man.

"But why?" she cried.

"That should be obvious," he said. "Oil, Catherine. Oil. All that black crude sitting under your land just waiting to be taken."

The answer hit Catherine with the physical force of a blow. The expression of growing horror on her face gave Devlin a contemptuous sort of courage that made him go on to reveal more than he had planned.

"My plan was a simple one, really. If the place went bankrupt, the bank would foreclose and offer it up at public auction. It would be easy enough to buy a worthless sheep ranch that no one else wanted.

Once I gained access to it and got rid of those miserable creatures, I could sink half a dozen wells all over the property. Of course, I never planned on you coming back to complicate things.

"Nor did I count on your tenacity. When you didn't turn tail and run, I had to revise my plan." His look hardened like the toughest drill bit and his gaze bored into her with equal intensity. "I knew then that I would have to destroy you."

The room was gripped in the strangling clutch of silence. Terror struck harsh chords in Catherine's heart at the awful confession.

"I got the idea to puncture the brake line of your car the day you brought that carcass to my office."

Her mind stumbled back to the day she'd driven into Edmonton. Yes, of course. He'd been alone with the car when he went outside to remove the carcass. She recalled having wondered what was taking him so long. Dear God, now she knew. She shuddered to think that she had actually suspected Ben guilty of negligence. Oh, how wrong she'd been!

"Not a full severing of the line, of course," he went on in that same cool, detached voice. "Just enough to allow the fluid to escape slowly, insuring that you wouldn't be able to brake rounding some of those narrow curves on your way home. Clever, don't you agree?"

Catherine was speechless, unable to respond even if she wanted to.

Devlin watched her features grow paler as he spoke, and reveled at the thought of bringing this proud, willful woman to her knees. Her horror only compounded his boldness, and with a lurid sense of truth, he admitted, "When cutting your brake line failed to work, I became quite desperate. All that oil and no way to get at it. When you began drilling on your own, I had to think of something quick. That's when it came to me. Without the well, you couldn't stay in business. I could also kill two birds with one stone, so to speak, by getting rid of Walker, too. I figured you got the money to drill from him, and didn't want to take the chance that he'd be around to give you more money to start over again."

Catherine was so terrified by what she was hearing that her skin quivered, but when he revealed his plans to hurt Cal, she forgot her own fear. Rushing up to him, she shouted, "You're insane! Money means so much to you that you would resort to murder? What kind of monster are you?"

Smugly, he replied, "A rich one. And about to become even richer."

"Not if I can help it," she seethed. "I'll go straight to the police with what you've just told me."

"Yes, well, I anticipated even that." He rose from the sofa and headed for the door. "My purpose here is finished, so if you'll excuse me, it's late and I have more planning to do."

He paused at the door to look back at her and add smugly, "Oh, by the way, after watching the well site from a distance for several days, I placed the dynamite charges where Walker was most likely to be, so I wouldn't count on him showing up, not tonight, anyway. Maybe not ever."

Hadn't she sensed something unsettling about him from the very beginning? She'd had no idea, however, that beneath the suave façade beat a sinister heart. The snake! He would never get his hands on her ranch. Not if she could help it! She was torn by the impulse to run straight to the authorities, but thought better of it. It was best to make sure that the vile man was gone before she acted.

But it was more than that which paralyzed Catherine's legs, making it impossible for her to act on her impulse. His cruel revelations had drained her, the guilt of having suspected Ben overwhelmed her, and the thought of having nearly lost Cal to that madman's schemes stripped her of her courage to move.

She realized with a start that Cal would not be coming. Where was he? What was so important that he had checked himself out of the hospital? She supposed she could wait here for him to return, which he would eventually do, but the poignant memories evoked earlier by these rooms had vanished, and she could think of nothing other than running as fast as she could from this house. Feeling she would burst with the knowledge she now carried, Catherine decided to go home and wait for Cal there.

She ran to the door and gave a cry of surprise to find it locked from the outside. What was that madman up to? She twisted the doorknob furiously without success. Her fingers shook treacherously as surprise turned to genuine fear. Suddenly, a familiar smell crept into her nostrils, stilling her frantic motions and driving a bolt of terror through her. It was the unmistakable smell of smoke.

Catherine stood perfectly still, barely breathing, her ear pressed up against the grainy surface for support. Beyond it, she could hear the spitting and crackling of the fire that was already into a full rage on the floors below, where the old furnishings and wide-planked wooden flooring and worn timbers proved good kindling.

In a matter of minutes the house was engulfed in flame. Pieces of structure crumbled beneath the diabolical pressure of the fire, landing on the lawn in blazing heaps. Sparks pierced the night like rockets in a fireworks display and flew into the treetops, setting aflame the tall pines surrounding the house. Stands of timber became like fiery sentries around the massive pyre that was the house.

Inside the blazing house, in the master bedroom on the third floor, a woman's frantic screams and cries for help were but a whisper compared to the bellow of the fire.

Catherine beat against the door with fists that grew weaker with each attempt. In a desperate rush she whirled around, spotted the window across the room, and staggered toward it.

"Oh, no!" The cry that was wrenched from her throat was part fright, part pain. Her already-parched throat was singed by the intake of heated air, but worse was the sight of all those flames licking the side of the house. To jump into that inferno was sure suicide.

Sealed off with no means of escape, fear and indignation battled for control of Catherine's rapidly dimming consciousness. Her hands tore at the buttons of her shirt in a vain attempt to get relief from the searing heat. She stumbled and landed on the floor. It was hot to the touch, blistering the flesh on her palms. Half-sobbing, half-choking she floundered around on her knees. Unholy fear clutched at her. Her strength melted like ice in the intense heat. At any moment the door would give way, and she would be swallowed up by the ravenous flames.

FOURTEEN

Cal drove like the devil was riding close behind. His bandaged hand throbbed mercilessly. The bruise at his temple was raw and aching. Every muscle in his body felt like it had been ripped in two. He felt weak and lightheaded from the concussion he had received in the explosion. But the urgency that tore at him was far, far worse than anything physical.

The pickup barreled into the gravel driveway and came to a screeching halt. Cal jumped down from the cab, leaving the door gaping open, and stomped up the porch steps, his fist all balled and ready to knock. He froze in mid-motion when he saw the note attached to the front door, the note that bore his signature and which he hadn't written.

"What the—?"

All the speculation surrounding Ben's crazy hunches vanished. It was more than either of them imagined. Spinning sharply on his boot heels he ran to the pickup and peeled out in the direction of Pitchfork.

Cal's furious thoughts stopped dead in their tracks when he saw the sky glowing red from the direction of his ranch. One word tore through his mind like a gunshot. *Fire*!

He arrived on the scene to find his home in flames. In a screech of brakes, he was out of the truck and running, running as fast as he could toward the burning building. His first thought was of Millie, but then he remembered giving her the weekend off and relief slammed into him that she was safe.

He stood on the front lawn watching the house that his grandfather had built being destroyed, feeling angry and frustrated and helpless to prevent it from happening, when a sound reached his ears. A scream, a woman's scream could be heard faintly above the roar of the flames. Cal went cold inside and a fear unlike anything he'd ever known exploded within him.

"Cathy!"

He raced around first to one side of the house, shouting her name up into the angry flames. Then to the other side, hoping to pinpoint exactly where she was. There it was again, another scream, fainter than the last, coming from the third floor. But where on the third floor? Which room? His own cries grew desperate. Then he saw it, the broken window panes of the third-floor bedroom. She must have shattered the glass in a vain attempt to escape.

Mindless of the danger, Cal rushed headlong into the burning house. The air inside was thick and black with smoke and as hot as hell itself. Beaten back by the flames, Cal stumbled back outside, gasping for air. Thinking quickly, he sprinted to the pickup and grasped the old blanket that was still there from the other day when he'd transported some equipment to the well site. At the pump he soaked it in water and hauled the heavy, sodden blanket back to the house. Wrapping himself in the wet blanket he forced his way back inside.

There was no way to get upstairs to reach her for the staircase was only a skeleton of its former self. He whirled around in all directions, trying to see through the black, biting smoke, dodging the flames that were everywhere. Then he remembered the back stairs off the kitchen. If there was any chance, no matter how slim, that they were intact, he had to find out.

The loss of the house was trivial compared to the prospect of losing Catherine. To have lost her once was bad enough, but to lose her again, and like this, was unthinkable. Gathering the blanket and his strength around him, Cal made a dash for the kitchen. He was coughing violently and gasping for breath, but when he saw the kitchen stairs still standing, he gave out with an involuntary cry.

The ravenous flames spared nothing on the second floor, but there was no time to survey the damage. Somehow, Cal made it to the second-floor bedroom that used to belong to his parents'. With strength borne of fury, he managed to push aside a flaming armoire to reveal a hidden passageway.

In his games of hide and seek with Catherine, he used to take unfair advantage of the passageway, using it in which to hide so that she could never find him and he could always win. Little did he know back then, when they were kids, to what use he would one day put this dark and dusty hallway that connected the second and third floors of the house.

* * *

Catherine lay in a small, terrified heap on the hot floor, still conscious, hoping she would faint so that her final moments would not be as painful as they promised to be. Through the daze that clouded her brain she could hear the beating on the door. The flames had reached her. At any moment now the door would burst open. *Oh, Cal,* she thought wretchedly. To have found him again and lost him. To have come so close and yet never know the happiness that awaited in his arms. But the worst pain imaginable came from knowing that she had not told him she loved him.

The pounding on the door increased. Any moment now . . . any moment and it would be all over. In that instant, when fear was at its most acute and hopelessness was at hand, Catherine thought she heard a voice call out to her. Her mind was playing cruel tricks on her. Oh God, she moaned, why did she have to imagine hearing Cal's voice at a time like this when it only made her dying that much more painful to endure?

Catherine looked up from where she lay crumpled on the floor and thought she saw his face. The smoke and heat were playing tricks on her sanity. She shut her eyes tightly.

She felt herself being pulled up from the floor and began to kick and scream, refusing to die quietly. Up, up into the air she went into the arms of the fire. It was only then that she lapsed into the dead faint she had prayed for.

There was a strange coolness beneath Catherine's cheek. By gradual degrees she became aware of her surroundings. She was alive. The air was clean and clear, no longer poisoned with smoke. Like a person gone mad, she gulped huge amounts of it into her scorched lungs.

Pushing herself up from the ground, Catherine looked up and gasped. In the distance the inferno still raged. Red flames licked the sky, illuminating the night for miles around. Catherine stared in stricken silence, unable at first to tell if this was really happening or if it was all a terrible nightmare.

Gradually, she became aware of a hand on her shoulder. A voice was speaking softly at her ear. Turning her gaze away from the house, Catherine gave a startled cry to find Cal kneeling beside her. His face was blackened with soot and smoke. His shirt was torn.

She opened her mouth but no sound emerged. All she could do was collapse into his arms and weep silent tears against his chest.

Cal hugged Catherine tightly to him, using the strength of his embrace to calm her. With an arm wrapped securely about her waist, he assisted her to her feet. In desperation they clung to each other, fearful of letting go. The raging bellow of the fire drowned out the wild beating of their hearts. Together, they watched in silence as Cal's house went through its final death throes. Within those crumbling walls Pitchfork history was going up in billows of thick, black smoke.

Cal turned Catherine away from the terrible sight just as the sound of sirens rose in the distance. From over the hillside, the cherry-red firetrucks sped to the scene. All hell broke lose as men rushed to and fro, shouting and scrambling to put out the fire. Cal shook his head with sad desperation. No matter how hard they tried, it was too late for the house.

"Oh, Cal," Catherine cried. "I'm so sorry. So sorry."

"Hey, babe," he said, trying his best to sound cavalier for her benefit, "it's only a house."

"No, not that. I'm sorry for not telling you how much I've always loved you. How much I still love you."

Her unexpected declaration rocked Cal down to his soul. He looked at her beautiful smoke-stained face, into those eyes that shined with courage in spite of her horrifying ordeal, and felt such an overwhelming love for her that for several moments he remained uncharacteristically at a loss for words. And then he said the only thing he could think of to say.

"And I love you. God, Cathy, sometimes I thought I'd die for loving you as much as I do."

"Can you ever forgive me?" she asked.

Gently, he replied, "There's nothing to forgive."

"I should have told you. I should have . . ." She began to cry, soft, silent tears spilling down her cheeks, making crooked little paths in the soot that covered her face.

"Shhh." He pulled her close to him and stroked her hair. "It's all right, Cath. I knew it all along."

She looked up at him, dark eyes all wet with tears. "You did?"

He smiled. "A woman doesn't make love the way you do unless she's in love." Through the darkness he saw the blush rise to her cheeks, and he only loved her more for it. "Although, I have to tell you, Cathy, I needed to hear it. I needed to hear it real bad. Especially now." He glanced over the top of her head toward the burning house.

Catherine felt him shudder and her heart cried out for his loss. "Cal?" The sound of her voice called him back to her. "There's something you must know. It was Drew Devlin who did this. It was him all along. He poisoned my sheep. He set the explosion at the well. He started this fire." She shuddered at the recollection that was still so fresh in her mind. "Oh, Cal, it was awful. The things he said. The things he did. All to get his hands on my land. It was the oil, Cal. All along, it was the oil."

She drew in a deep breath to steel herself against the perfidy and deception to which they had both been subjected, first by her father and then by the man who had tried to destroy them both.

In a voice that was scarcely a whisper Cal said, "I know about Devlin."

Confusion clouded Catherine's eyes. "But how?"

"Come on," he said gently, "let's get away from this mess and I'll explain everything to you."

He led her to a grove of sweet-smelling pines that was far enough away from the house to have been unharmed by the flames, and pulled her down to the ground beside him. With her back pressed up against the trunk of the tree, Cal's arm wrapped tightly about her shoulder, Catherine sat there for many long minutes without speaking while Cal told her about the phone call he had received from Ben.

When Catherine finally found the strength to speak, she asked in a small voice, "What do you think will happen to Devlin now?"

Cal's solid bulk tensed with anger. "We'll let the authorities deal with that miserable . . . with him."

Although, Cal seethed inwardly, if it were up to him, he would have broken every bone in Devlin's body, not for what the bastard did to him, but for what he'd done to Cathy. Just as he would deal similarly with anyone who ever tried to hurt her again.

"Oh God," Catherine groaned, "To think how I misjudged Ben. Gertie was right. Ben *is* a good man." She looked at Cal with an anxious expression troubling her beautiful, soot-stained face and asked, "Do you think Ben will ever forgive me?"

Cal smiled tenderly and suggested, "I think an apology might do it."

"An apology! I'll do better than that. I'm going to offer Ben a partnership in the ranch." In answer to the stunned expression on Cal's face her chin shot up defiantly. "Why not? He deserves it. It must have been awful for him sharing the management of the ranch with me after he'd been doing it for six years without my help. Damn, but I can be such a fool at times."

She caught the knowing roll of Cal's eyes and the concurring smile and poked him hard in the ribs with her elbow. "That's enough out of you, Calvin Walker."

But when he grunted with pain, she quickly threw her arms around his neck, saying between the kisses that she covered his face with, "I'm so sorry. Did I hurt you? Let me make it better."

His lips were waiting and parted to receive her kiss. The heat of his mouth was more intense than any flame had ever been and threatened to burn her to cinders. But it was a sweet, exquisite kind of torture that made Catherine press her slender body against the hardness of his. With the meeting of their lips came the sealing of their love, an unspoken sureness that had endured in spite of everything.

Catherine broke away and ventured breathlessly, "Would you do something for me, Cal?"

His heart beat frantically within his breast. "For you, Cathy, I'd do anything."

"Drive me to the point. You know the place I mean."

"Right now?"

"Right now."

He grasped her hand and pulled her lightly to her feet. "Come on then, let's go."

They left the fire engines and the flames and the chaos behind and drove to the place they both knew so well. Dawn was tinting the horizon when they got there. They alit from the pickup truck and walked hand in hand to the end of the point. For many moments they stood there staring in wordless wonder at the panorama spread out thousands of feet below. In the distance the saw-toothed peaks of the magnificent Rockies disappeared into the clouds.

Cal used Catherine's serenity to study her. Ribbons of early-morning sunlight danced in her hair, setting the dark tresses aglow. Her profile etched against the brightening sky was beautiful to behold. With her beauty, warmth, and courage she had become a treasure that the years had not diminished in his eyes. In a word, she was all to him.

For Catherine, where the green-eyed cattleman was concerned, one underlying truth prevailed. She loved him. More than she had ever loved any man. She thought of his confession of how much he needed to hear it, and cupping her hands to her mouth, she shouted into the breathtaking stillness.

"I love you, Calvin Walker!"

The echo of Catherine's declaration bounced off the canyon walls and ricocheted off the hillsides again and again, until the whole world knew how very much she loved him.

A joyous, exultant feeling shook Cal hard. How he had longed to hear those words. He swept her into his arms. "There's not a thing about you that I would change," he whispered into her ear. "Except your name." He smiled impishly and said, "You were always meant to be a Walker, and I aim to make you one."

The love and concern Catherine saw radiating from those clear green eyes thrilled her as much as the promise of being this man's wife. She tossed her head back and laughed huskily. "I thought you'd never ask."

They walked hand in hand back to the truck, giddy as two kids over the prospect of forever. Like an echo shouted by the heart, their love had resounded off the walls of the past and found its way back home.

SHARE THE FUN . . .
SHARE YOUR NEW-FOUND TREASURE!!

You don't want to let your new books out of your sight? That's okay. Your friends can get their own. Order below.

No. 25 LOVE WITH INTEREST by Darcy Rice
Stephanie & Elliot find $47,000,000 *plus* interest—true love!

No. 26 NEVER A BRIDE by Leanne Banks
The last thing Cassie wanted was a relationship. Joshua had other ideas.

No. 27 GOLDILOCKS by Judy Christenberry
David and Susan join forces and get tangled in their own web.

No. 28 SEASON OF THE HEART by Ann Hammond
Can Lane and Maggie's newfound feelings stand the test of time?

No. 29 FOSTER LOVE by Janis Reams Hudson
Morgan comes home to claim his children but Sarah claims his heart.

No. 30 REMEMBER THE NIGHT by Sally Falcon
Joanna throws caution to the wind. Is Nathan fantasy or reality?

No. 31 WINGS OF LOVE by Linda Windsor
Mac & Kelly soar to new heights of ecstasy. Are they ready?

No. 32 SWEET LAND OF LIBERTY by Ellen Kelly
Brock has a secret and Liberty's freedom could be in serious jeopardy!

No. 33 A TOUCH OF LOVE by Patricia Hagan
Kelly seeks peace and quiet and finds paradise in Mike's arms.

No. 34 NO EASY TASK by Chloe Summers
Hunter is wary when Doone delivers a package that will change his life.

No. 35 DIAMOND ON ICE by Lacey Dancer
Diana could melt even the coldest of hearts. Jason hasn't a chance.

No. 36 DADDY'S GIRL by Janice Kaiser
Slade wants more than Andrea is willing to give. Who wins?

No. 37 ROSES by Caitlin Randall
It's an inside job & K.C. helps Brett find more than the thief!

No. 38 HEARTS COLLIDE by Ann Patrick
Matthew finds big trouble and it's spelled P-a-u-l-a.

No. 39 QUINN'S INHERITANCE by Judi Lind
Gabe and Quinn share an inheritance and find an even greater fortune.

No. 40 CATCH A RISING STAR by Laura Phillips
Justin is seeking fame; Beth helps him find something more important.